SUNSET DREAMS

JILL SANDERS

GRAYTON

To my walking & axe-throwing friends,
Amelia & Sarah

SUMMARY

Clara Cruz has spent the last five years on the run, most of the time hiding in plain sight, blending into the background so as not to cause unwanted attention. Being invisible is necessary if she wants to survive, but the loneliness and isolation have proved more difficult than anticipated. Successful thus far, everything changes abruptly when she finds herself running straight into the arms of the man sent to find her.

Giving that Reagan Grayton had spent most of his childhood hiding from a crazy cult-leading biological grandfather, it was only natural that he'd end up in a career searching for missing people. However, with his latest case, things just aren't adding up. A pretty brunette heiress has been accused of murder. Trouble is, she just doesn't seem like the murdering type. As things take a bizarre turn, he finds himself caught up in a sinister plot. He may have found his missing person, but now he'll be lucky to escape with his life.

PROLOGUE

Twenty years ago…

Seven-year-old Reagan stood and watched his mother walking slowly across the white sugar-soft sand towards them.

He chanced a glance up at the man that had found them a few weeks ago, his father. He had a dad! Finally.

He and his mother had been hiding all of his life from his biological grandfather, who had been head of a cult called the Council of Friends, a silly name for such a scary group. They believed his grandfather was their messiah, come to earth to lead them to the promised land. What did that even mean, anyway?

When his mother stopped directly in front of them, his father reached down and squeezed his shoulder and smiled down at him. His hair was long, and Reagan had already memorized his tan face.

"You sure about this, buddy?" he asked softly, a smile playing on his lips, so much like the one Reagan saw in the mirror every morning.

"Hell, yeah!" he answered loudly, causing the small group gathered around them to chuckle.

"You've been hanging around your uncles too much." His father, Roman Grayton, frowned down at him, then glanced over to where his three uncles sat, smiling proudly at them.

"Naw." He chuckled. "I learned everything I know from my mother."

His mother, Marissa Grayton, laughed. The soft white dress she was wearing flowed in the gentle breeze coming off the Gulf of Mexico. She turned to the older man who had raised both of his parents after adopting them at a young age.

"Thanks, Dad." She leaned up and kissed the paper-thin skin on the man's cheek.

His new grandfather—not the one who had just tried to kill him less than a week ago—smiled down at him and winked. "Welcome to the family, grandson." He squeezed his shoulder, much like his father had just done.

Reagan thought he saw a tear slip down the old man's cheek before he turned around and sat with the rest of the wedding party on the beach.

He tried—really, he did—to pay attention to the wedding vows. After all, he was acting as his father's best man. He had responsibilities. Not to mention that his parents were officially getting married.

But his mind began to wander, and he caught himself glancing towards the clear emerald water just a few feet away from him. He wished he had his board shorts on and could jump in and enjoy a day at the beach with his family. He had a family!

He thought about his new life. All of his aunts and

uncles had been adopted by Mark and Elizabeth Grayton after each of them had been rescued from the personal hell of their biological homes by Lilly, a caseworker. His mother often described her as an angel, but she sat in the second row, watching the wedding with tears in her eyes, and didn't look much like an angel. She was an older woman who reminded him of his second-grade teacher.

Even though his parents had been raised as brother and sister since being adopted by the Graytons, they technically had no blood relation.

His mother had always told him that, from the moment she'd seen Rowan when she'd first arrived at the Grayton's large home in a town called Spring Haven, she'd known she loved him.

For the last few years, his mother and he had been hiding in another small town, just down the coast from where his family had been. Carrabelle was the only home he remembered. He'd found out that his father hadn't even known he'd existed. His mother, shortly after finding out she was pregnant at seventeen, had received a visit from her mother, who had warned her that her father had found her.

His mother had run, but it had been too late. His grandfather had captured her. But after Reagan's birth, when his grandfather had been proclaimed the group's messiah, they had escaped with her mother's help. His mother had hidden them away, always protecting him. But now, they were done hiding.

For years, his mother had run a small store in Carrabelle, but his parents had decided that, after getting married, they would move closer to their family.

He hated the idea of starting a new school but was

excited about spending more time with his uncles and aunts.

He focused again when he heard his name being said.

Turning to his parents, he took in the sling still on his father's arm. Reagan and his mom had been kidnapped once more by his biological grandfather, and Roman had gotten shot saving Reagan as they escaped.

"We wanted you to be part of this." His father smiled down at him, and he focused. "We both promise you that, no matter what happens, you will always be safe here." Rowan glanced around the small group. "This is your family and the Graytons protect each other."

"Here, here." Several cheers rang out from the group.

He turned his eyes to his mother. She'd explained that she'd been a stupid seventeen-year-old girl when she'd left these people, afraid that her father would find her and take her away again. Part of him wished that he had been alive back then to protect her and convince her to stick with her family.

Still, everything was going to be all right now. Now that they had been found, he knew that no matter what life threw at them, they could deal with it together.

His biological grandfather was locked away for good this time. He ran his eyes over his new family and knew that nothing would ever come between them again.

"Welcome to the family," his uncle shouted out.

His mother leaned down until they were eye to eye. "You've always been part of the family," she smiled. "But we are finally home."

"It's official, you're a Grayton now." His dad pulled him and his mother into a hug.

Reagan thought that he wanted to stay there, warm and

safe in his family's arms, forever. Someday, he would help others to get what he now had. Someday, he would protect those who couldn't protect themselves. Find the lost, like his father had.

His father was the biggest hero in his eyes, and he wanted nothing more than to grow up and be just like him. Someday.

CHAPTER 1

eagan watched the pretty brunette from across the room. She looked comfortable with the heavy tray of drinks balanced over her head on one hand, which made him question if he had the right woman.

He was looking for an heiress, not a waitress. He pulled out his cell phone and glanced down at the grainy image once again. The picture was more than five years old and looked like it had been scanned at one point. Still, as he squinted and watched her handing out the drinks, he could tell it was the same woman. Her hair was shorter, and she wasn't a thin teenager anymore. His eyes moved to the tight tank top she was wearing, and a smile of appreciation flashed quickly and was gone before anyone could see it.

He'd spent the last few years of his life looking for the lost. Before that, he'd done the same thing during a short stint in the Special Forces, but he'd been medically discharged years before he was ready to leave after he'd gotten hurt saving a few men on his team who'd been pinned down during a rescue mission.

His lower back and left thigh still gave him pain when he found himself in cooler climates. But now, he leaned back and nursed the single beer he'd ordered and watched the waves outside of the restaurant's windows. Being back in the Panhandle was pure heaven.

That a job had brought him so close to home had been pure luck, but something hadn't sat well with him from the moment he'd taken the job. It wasn't the old man who'd hired him but the fact that the guy didn't seem to have any idea where his daughter was or why she'd left in the first place. Who waits five years to look for their kid?

He thought of his own father, whom he'd met for the first time when he was seven. But that wasn't his dad's fault. Hell, the man hadn't even known he'd had a son until after he'd met him, and his parents had gotten married shortly after. Not a day had gone by since then that he hadn't talked to his father.

He focused back on his job and sized up the woman as she took a young tourist's order.

Clara Cruz, current age twenty-five, the older of the two daughters of one of the wealthiest real estate moguls in southern California. She was last seen over five years ago at a graduation party for her younger sister, Gina, who had been brutally murdered in their father's den that night. Clara had been found hovering over her sister's body, her party dress soaked in blood. She'd claimed that she had no memory of what had happened. She'd been carted in and questioned but had been released.

To his knowledge, no reason had been given for why

she hadn't been charged with her sister's murder. His best guess was that her father had friends in the court system.

Still, the woman had disappeared from the family's life shortly after her release, and it was only now that they wanted to look for her. Why?

Was it guilt that had her running? It wasn't his job to find out, but he was curious enough to have spent the last two days returning to the restaurant she worked at to watch her.

He'd found the woman; his job was over. All he had to do was make a phone call and get paid. Then why was he second-guessing doing so?

She moved closer to his table and when their eyes locked, he felt his body respond to the sexy way her dark eyebrows drew up slowly as she approached him.

"Are you still okay?" she asked, her voice soft and warm, which only caused his body to react even more.

"Yes." He nodded to his half-full beer.

Instead of moving away, she leaned a hip on his table. "You've come in the past two evenings." It was a statement, not a question. "Nursing a beer and watching me." Her eyes narrowed. "I can't tell if you're some sort of stalker or…" She dropped off.

He pasted on the most innocent smile he could muster. "Just enjoying the view," he said, then he slowly nodded to the beach just to his left.

"Where are you from?" she asked as her eyes ran up and down him quickly.

"Here and there." He shrugged.

"Military?" she asked quickly. When he raised his eyebrows, she added, "The base is just twenty miles away."

"Used to be," he said honestly.

"You're too young to be retired."

"Medical discharge." He didn't know why he was answering her questions when he had more than a dozen for her himself.

"Clara." She waved to herself. "You?"

"Reagan," he answered.

"Nice to meet you, Reagan." She leaned closer to him. "If you don't order something more, I'll have to send my boss Rico over here." She nodded over her shoulder to a very large man behind the bar, who happened to be glaring at him at the moment. "He's been dying to send you on your way since you first walked in here."

He chuckled at that. Sure, the man was probably big enough to send him packing, but Reagan knew size was only half of what mattered. Rico may look like a protective giant, but Reagan had watched the man the past two nights and knew that the guy kept his two dachshunds behind the bar with him. The man was a softy on the inside.

Reagan shifted slightly, bringing his body closer to hers. "Is he going to sick Princess and Duchess on me?" he asked, using the dog's names.

Clara smiled and he felt his heart skip at the beautiful transformation, something he hadn't felt in years.

"He may look like a softy, but I assure you, Rico could clear a room."

He laughed again. "I wouldn't doubt it." He tilted his head. "How about we compromise?"

Her eyebrows shot up again. "I'm all ears."

"Agree to meet me after you get off, and I'll order the most expensive item on the menu."

The change in her was quick. She took a step away from him and her entire body tensed.

"I don't date customers," she said quickly.

"Who said anything about dating." He watched her close up even further, her eyes darting around the room, then resting back on him.

"Sip your beer." She took another step away. "I'll bring you a basket of fries." She turned and walked away without another word.

He wasn't surprised when the basket of fries was delivered by Rico, who glared hard at him as he set the basket down with a thump.

"She's not interested," the big man said, then he lowered his voice. "You'd be wise to find someplace else to enjoy your beers for the remainder of your stay."

Reagan watched the man walk back to the bar and appreciated the guy for looking out for his employees.

Leaving the beer and the fries, he tossed a crisp bill on the table and strolled out of the bar.

Sitting in his truck, he watched the bar until the open sign flickered off. He should have made the call. He'd told himself that more than a hundred times since he'd first laid eyes on her.

Why hadn't he then?

All of the other employees left, and he waited in the dark until Clara and Rico walked out of the restaurant together, the two small dogs in tow behind the larger man. They stopped, talked for a moment, then hugged quickly before he turned and helped the little ones into a massive black Jeep.

She climbed behind the wheel of a beat-up Ford sedan.

The Jeep pulled out of the parking lot quickly while the Ford remained in its spot.

He frowned when he noticed her getting out of the car and looking under the hood. He was just about to jump out and see if he could help her, when he spotted movement a few feet behind her.

Clara kicked the tire of the secondhand car she'd bought with her first three paychecks. She'd finally saved up enough to buy new tires and now she apparently needed a new battery as well.

"Stupid thing, why couldn't you have given me some warning?" She groaned as she kicked the tire again and felt pain shoot up her ankle.

It had been hard keeping her mind on her work after Reagan had left. She'd been thankful Rico had told her to take her break and had dealt with the sexy man instead of her.

For the past two days she'd thought of little else. Of course, she'd seen her fair share of men come and go in the restaurant. After all, she'd chosen one of the busiest places along the Florida coast to work at, since she needed enough money to keep hiding.

She blocked thoughts of her past before they consumed her. Leaning in, she jiggled the battery wires in hopes that they were just lose. When the red one came off in her hand, she smiled. She put it back on, so focused on making it stay put that she didn't notice the dark figure coming up behind her until it was too late to protect herself. But before he could grab her, another figure rushed forward from the opposite direction and took down the first.

A squeal escaped her lips and she quickly backed up, bumping the front of the car. The hood of her Ford came crashing down, scraping her back. She watched in horror as the two dark figures wrestled across the gravel parking lot.

She had just turned to get back into the safety of her car when she heard a gunshot. Her entire body froze. She heard pounding footsteps as the first figure disappeared into the darkness. She turned towards the lone remaining figure on the ground as the other man disappeared around the corner of the building.

She turned to run, something she should have thought of doing in the first few seconds. But then she heard someone say, "Son of a..."

She paused. She knew that voice.

"Reagan?" She took a step forward, but it was dark, and she worried that she'd heard wrong. The dark mass on the ground grunted.

"Yeah, want to help a guy out? After all, I did just save you from... whatever the hell that was." He grunted.

She reached in her pocket and pulled out her cell phone, then flipped on the flashlight mode. Sure enough, Reagan was sitting on the pavement, holding his head in his hands. A gun sat in his lap.

"Are you shot?" she asked, moving closer to him.

"It just scraped me," he answered and moved his hands away from his neck. His shirt was splattered lightly with blood around his collar and she gasped.

"You are shot." She rushed to his side, unsure of how to help.

"I'm fine." He replaced his hand over the area, blocking her view of how bad it was. "Any idea who that was?" he asked quickly.

"Who?" She held her phone's light up to his neck, trying to get a better look.

"The guy that just shot me after trying to…"—he shrugged— "kidnap or attack you?"

"No." She frowned. "Maybe it was a mugger. This is a big vacation spot. People come and go. Last month, my car was broken into." She glanced around. "Do you think he left?"

"Yeah, he's gone." Reagan sighed and started to get up, tucking the gun into his pants.

"What do you think you're doing?" She gasped. "You need a hospital. I'm calling—"

He stopped her by putting a hand on her elbow.

"I'm fine," he repeated.

"I can drive you…" She stopped when she realized that her car still may not work.

"No. I'm fine. I've had worse." He stood up and glanced around, and she realized how much taller he was than she'd imagined. He'd always been sitting when she'd seen him before. Now he was standing next to her, and she also realized that his shoulders were wide, and his arms were thicker than her thighs. The man was a tank, and her knees went a little weak. He ignored her assessment of his form and asked, "What's wrong with your car?" He motioned with his head.

She followed his gaze, unable to switch her train of thought that quickly. Focusing her eyes on her dead car, she sighed. "The battery, I think."

"I'll take a look."

She stopped him by yanking on his arm, or tried to anyway, since she couldn't have budged him at all. "You were just shot."

"Scratched," he corrected. "Literally." He showed her the area. Sure enough, there was a long red scrape mark that ran across his skin just below his left ear. There was still blood dripping from it, but it wasn't as bad as she'd imagined. "I'm fine."

"But…" She bit her bottom lip and thought about how close it had been.

"Let's have a look at your car." He moved over to her hood and she followed him, her eyes returning to his neck.

"That should be cleaned and bandaged," she said as he leaned into her car.

"Later." He blew her concern off as he concentrated on fixing her car.

When he stood up abruptly, he almost bumped into her, since she'd crowded near him to look over his shoulder.

"What is it?" she asked after seeing his frown.

"Your cables were disconnected," he answered.

"They were disconnected. I was trying to put them back on."

"No." He shook his head. "Here, they were disconnected down here as well." He turned back and aimed his cell phone light at the bottom of the battery. Now she could see it clearly. The cables were unhooked farther down. Even if she had reconnected them above, her car wouldn't have started.

Feeling defeated, she leaned on the hood. "Now what do I do?"

He stepped back and shut the hood of her car. "Now I

drive you home, and you get a mechanic out here in the morning to fix this."

"You don't think…" She glanced to the dark corner where the man who had almost jumped her had disappeared. She felt a shiver rush down her back. She wrapped her arms around herself and held on.

"Yeah." Reagan sighed, interrupting her thoughts. "Yes, I do."

CHAPTER 2

*T*he silence inside his truck cab stretched on. He knew Clara was thinking about what had happened.

It had taken some convincing to get her to trust him enough to allow him to drive her to her place. It was less than two miles, but after he'd hinted that whoever had unhooked her cables wouldn't stop just because he'd thwarted the attack in the parking lot, she'd quickly agreed.

When he pulled into the small condo complex where she rented and shut of the engine, she glanced up at her place on the second floor and blinked a few times. Then she turned towards him.

"You should really clean that." She motioned to his neck. He'd forgotten about the scratch already. The dried blood caked and pulled at his skin when he turned his head. She was right, he needed to clean himself up. But first, he had to make sure she was safe.

He should have called her family the moment he'd

found her and moved on to another job. Now he'd have a full night ahead of him, watching her place to make sure whoever had tried to get to her earlier didn't try again.

He thought of a way to convince her to let him come inside and was just about to ask when she jumped in.

"Why don't you come in and let me clean that for you?" She reached for the door handle. "It's the least I can do for you saving me."

He didn't hesitate and rushed around to hold the passenger truck door open for her. She stepped out of the truck and her eyes ran over him slowly, as if she was trying to figure him out. Then they zeroed in on his face.

"You're bleeding again." She motioned to his neck. Reaching up, he touched the spot where the bullet had grazed him and winced when his fingers came away wet. "Come on in." She stepped around him, and he followed her up the dark pathway towards the cement stairwell.

"Nice place," he said as they climbed the stairs while he scanned the darkness surrounding them. The condos sat directly above businesses in a small shopping area that was filled with tourists and locals during the day. Now, however, it was past midnight and it was abandoned. He made sure whoever had tried to attack her wasn't hiding in the shadows, ready to spring on them as she unlocked the door.

When she stepped inside her door and flipped on the lights, he followed her in and turned the lock on the door behind him. He knew it wouldn't keep anyone out if they were determined to get in. They could simply kick the wood door down. Still, the sound of it would give him plenty of warning.

He studied her small one-room condo. It was your

normal tourist rental, even down to the pastel furniture and flamingo paintings.

"Rental?" he asked.

"Yes," she said over her shoulder as she walked towards the bathroom just off the main room. "Fully furnished. I got a good deal on it…" She stopped herself and shook her head. "Let's just say, come morning, you won't be able to sleep in." He realized that directly under her place was the local coffee and bagel shop, which was one of the busiest businesses in the area. She shrugged as she flipped on the bathroom light and started looking through her medicine cabinet. "Why don't you come in here?" She motioned to him. "We can clean you up." She held a bottle of hydrogen peroxide and a clean cloth.

He tossed off his light jacket and threw it over the back of the sofa, then moved into the small bathroom with her.

Instantly, he felt huge in the small space.

"Wow, I've never really thought of this place as small," she said as she started using the wet cloth to clean up most of the blood. Then her eyes locked on his. "Until you came in."

He chuckled, then winced when the cloth brushed over the cut.

"Sorry," she hissed lightly.

"It's fine." He watched her as she worked on cleaning him up.

"So, ex-military…" She let her question hang in the air.

"Yes," he answered after a moment.

"What do you do now?" she asked. He'd known the question was coming and had worked out an answer that was true enough.

"Odd jobs." He shrugged.

"As in?" She met his gaze.

"This or that," he answered, but her eyes narrowed. "Contract work."

"As in construction?" She wet a fresh cloth with the peroxide. "This might sting," she warned, then dabbed the cut with the cloth.

He sucked in his breath as she worked cleaning him up, but it didn't have anything to do with the peroxide.

She smelled so good. How did someone who had just worked ten hours at a bar and restaurant smell like flowers?

He leaned closer to her, just to get a better chance of having her scent cling to him.

"So?" she said after a moment.

His eyebrows rose as he focused on her face again. He'd been watching her lips. They were full and when she concentrated, she bit her bottom lip. Which had him thinking of kissing it, taking it into his own mouth and nibbling on the soft skin. Sucking it until she—

"Reagan?" She shook him. "You're not in shock, are you?" She was frowning at him.

"No, I'm fine," he answered. She relaxed slightly and set down the cloth.

"I don't think a bandage will help. I have these." She held up small butterfly Band-Aids. "They might stay on until you shave in the morning." She shrugged.

He took the bandages from her and tucked them into his jean pocket. "If I need them, I'll use them," he said, his eyes returning to her lips.

"You never answered me." She leaned against the countertop.

"No, not construction. Just odd jobs. Whatever my clients need."

Her frown increased. "That sounds like a…" She bit her lip again, and he found it hard to focus once more. "You aren't a gigolo, are you?"

He burst out laughing. "No." She smiled back at him. "No, I'm not a male prostitute."

She relaxed a little and tilted her head as she looked at him once more. "You've got blood all over your shirt."

His smile was back. "Trying to get me naked?"

She shrugged and gave him a slight smile. "Maybe."

He moved closer to her, shrinking the space between them. "What is it about you?" he asked just before he set his hands on her hips and nudged her the rest of the way until her chest bumped against his.

"I… haven't done this in a—"

He stopped her by covering those full lips he'd been thinking about since he'd first laid eyes on her. She tasted even better than she smelled.

Whatever happened now, he knew that this wasn't going to be the easy missing person's case he'd hoped for. There was no way Clara Cruz was going to get away from him until he knew her entire story.

What was she doing? Flirting with and kissing a man she didn't know. A man who very well could have been the one who had unhooked her battery cables.

Then his lips touched hers and her mind stopped working as her body took over completely.

She wasn't lying. It had been a while since she'd

allowed herself any sort of pleasure. It had been over five years since she'd been touched intimately. No kisses, no hand-holding, no sex. She needed to stay focused if she was going to remain a free woman, even if it meant pulling away from the first man she'd desired.

The way he'd looked at her at the restaurant had turned her knees weak and made her insides feel like they were on fire. Two nights ago, when he'd walked into Rico's Beach Hut, the attraction between them had been instant.

She'd thought herself lucky when he'd returned the following night. But when he'd continued to watch her and sip his beer, she'd felt unnerved. Rico had instantly warned her about the man.

Then again, Rico didn't like anyone that came sniffing around his family. The man took care of his employees, which was one of the reasons she found herself staying in Paradise Cove longer than any other place she'd lived in the past five years. She felt safe, which was why someone had gotten close enough to her that Reagan had almost been shot.

Maybe he was behind the attack. Maybe he and a buddy had set the whole thing up.

She tensed and jerked away from him. Her eyes locked with his, and her mind sharpened. He'd left the restaurant almost an hour before closing.

"What were you still doing in the parking lot of the Hut?" she asked, her breath coming in deep gushes, much like it always did when she felt she was in danger.

"Waiting for you," he said easily. "I wanted to…" He sighed. "I wanted to give you a second chance to go out with me."

She didn't know why, but the obvious lie made her relax. "Liar."

"I need a drink," He glanced into the kitchen. "Got anything strong in there?"

She thought about the bottle of wine she had planned on enjoying while binge-watching the rest of her favorite show.

"Strong? Not really. I do have a bottle of wine."

"That will do." He motioned for her to step out of the bathroom, then followed her into her kitchen.

He stood back as she pulled out two plastic glasses and then a bottle of cheap wine from the fridge. It wasn't much, but she'd learned to enjoy what she could in the past few years.

She felt him watching her and, somehow, her body vibrated with want even more.

She'd never been the kind of person who lived for danger and thrills. She had been the girl who always stayed on the pathway. In school, she'd been an honor student, which had gained her entry into one of the best colleges in California. She'd believed her father when he'd told her that he hadn't paid her way into Stanford. She'd also played by the rules with boys, always choosing the safe route, the boys from quality families, never the partier types. Even though she'd daydreamed about men like Reagan all of her life, she'd dated the scrawny nerd types.

Her eyes moved to Reagan again. It was no wonder the man was setting off her sex drive. He was her fantasy man come to life: tall, masculine, dangerous, and mysterious. Everything she'd been taught to avoid growing up, yet just what she'd wanted.

That kiss in the bathroom had been more exciting than

any sexual experience she'd had before. Hell, all of her fumbled sexual encounters together couldn't equal the amount of desire she'd felt during that brief kiss with Reagan.

She bit her bottom lip and tried to convince herself that she would be better off shoving him out of her tiny apartment. If there was one thing that she'd learned from the past few years, it was that you opened yourself up too much when you started trusting others.

Instead of making him leave, she turned to him and handed him a plastic glass full of cheap wine.

CHAPTER 3

*W*ho the hell was she? From what Reagan had learned about her, the woman standing in front of him had been born with a silver spoon in her mouth. Yet, as he watched her pour the wine into two plastic glasses, she moved and acted as if it was the most natural thing in the world to her. As if she was pouring the most expensive champagne into Waterford Crystal flutes instead.

When she handed him his glass, their eyes met, and her eyes narrowed.

"What?" She frowned as she sipped her wine and moved to lean against the counter.

"Why would someone want to attack you?" He set the glass down without taking a drink, her eyes tracking his movement.

"Why does any man want to attack a woman in a dark parking lot," she answered easily, but he noticed a slight shiver race through her.

He moved closer. "For what it's worth, I doubt he was

there to rape you."

"Oh?" Her dark eyebrows rose. "What makes you say that?"

"He…" He swallowed. How could he tell her his thoughts without blowing his cover? "Intuition."

"Do you have much experience with rapists then?" she said between sips.

"Some," he answered honestly. "Something tells me he had other intentions."

"Are you a cop?" she asked, ignoring his reaction, and he saw her tense.

"No." He sighed and relaxed. "Like I said…"

"You're a contractor." She finished her drink, keeping her eyes on him. "Yet you haven't explained exactly what that means."

"I… do what I did tonight." He figured it would be easiest if he was vague. "Protect people."

She was silent for a moment as her eyes scanned him. "Like a bodyguard?"

He relaxed. "Something like that."

"So, if it wasn't rape… what then? Why would someone attack me? I have less than a hundred dollars in my checking account. My tips from tonight were shit…" She trailed off and he could see she was trying to keep her past from him. The worry that her life had caught up with her was obvious.

"You tell me?" He leaned against the countertop and watched her closely.

She bit her bottom lip, and he could tell she was thinking of how to avoid answering the line of questions she had started.

"What about your family?" he asked, steering her.

She shook her head. "No, I have no one who would be looking for me," she answered quickly, then sucked in a breath when she realized what she'd given away.

"Looking?" he asked. "As in, they don't know where you are?"

"No." She turned around and poured some more wine into her glass and looked out the window as she drank. "I'm on my own." She shrugged. "Have been for a while."

"Must be lonely," he said, thinking of his own large family. His mind flashed to his aunts and uncles and his younger sister, Bella, who was starting her second year of college in Arizona.

Even though his parents had been adopted into the same home as brother and sister, they had never thought of themselves as such. On his eighth birthday, almost a full year after they had come together finally as a family, his mother had given birth to his sister.

Mark Grayton, his grandfather, a man Reagan had grown to look up to almost as much as his father, was still as frail looking as the day that he'd met him all those years ago. He still lived in the big house, with his daughter, Julie, a great-aunt who had spoiled Reagan as a child and still called him on a weekly basis.

"It can be." Something close to pain crossed her face before she turned away.

"You do have family, though, right?" he asked, unsure why he was pressing her.

"Some," she said softly. She straightened her shoulders and turned back to him. "I have to get up early, you know, to arrange to have my car fixed."

"Right." He nodded. "I don't suppose you work again tomorrow night?"

He could see fear leap into her dark eyes. She swallowed. "I do, until closing again."

He nodded again. "I'll see you then. This time, I'll stay until closing."

He watched her relax. "You'd do that?" She frowned.

He leaned closer to her and whispered. "It's what I do." Then, without giving her time to move away, he laid another gentle kiss on her, taking a moment to enjoy the softness of her lips before moving away and letting himself out of her apartment.

He heard the door click as she locked it behind him and smiled.

As he jogged down the stairs, trying to act like nothing more than a man interested in a girl, his eyes scanned the darkness and spotted the sedan sitting across the parking lot.

He wouldn't have noticed it except for the movement behind the dark glass. Avoiding it, he got behind the wheel of his truck and pulled out of the parking lot. He circled the building and parked less than a block away.

He pulled on his dark hoodie, tucked his registered firearm into the hip holster he wore, then quietly made his way back to the parking lot.

He doubted whoever it was would make a move before Clara turned off the lights of the apartment, so he had plenty of time to get into position.

When the man finally exited the car, almost a full hour later, he was there, waiting for him. He didn't see what was coming next and, this time, it was Reagan who had the upper hand.

～

Clara stood back and watched the older man and his son hoist up her car to tow it away.

"Are you sure it can't be fixed here?" she asked again. She knew that the last hundred dollars in her account wouldn't come close to covering both the fee of fixing the battery cables and the tow truck costs.

The older man turned towards her, his eyes shifting a little. "As I said, the cables are too far down for us to connect here. We have to get her up on the lift to get under her." The fact that the man kept referring to her car as female slightly irritated her. Especially when he called it an "old girl" once. The fact that she could easily see the ends of the cables and where they should be connected had her questioning him.

"Yeah, but…" She bit her bottom lip.

"Is there a problem?" a deep voice said from behind her. She turned and felt all of the sexual tension from last night return in one quick swoosh as Reagan moved over to her side. "Sorry I'm late, honey." He bent down and kissed her quickly, before turning his eyes up to the two men.

"I was just telling the missus that we have to bring this old girl in to repair the cables," the older man jumped in.

"Why?" Reagan asked easily. "The cables are easily accessed." He popped her hood release, opened the hood of her car, and glanced in. "I could probably do it myself"—he shifted a glance at the two men— "if I had the tools." He motioned to the tool box in the back of the man's tow truck.

"Listen, buddy, we know our job…" the younger man started but was quickly hushed by his father.

"You wouldn't be trying to get the extra tow fee out of us, would you?" Reagan crossed his arms over his chest.

"Because I'm sure the BBB would be very interested in hearing about this. Not to mention, a quick review on Yelp could have you hurting for business around here. I passed several other auto shops on the way over here. I'm sure any of them would be happy—"

"We can fix it," the older man interrupted. He turned and grabbed his tool box, then motioned for his son to remove the tow ropes while he bent over the hood of the car.

"Thank you," Clara said softly when Reagan moved to her side.

"I figured I would check to see if you needed any help." He turned to her and ran his eyes over her face, causing her knees to turn to jelly.

He looked tired and he was still wearing the same shirt under his dark jacket. Did he have a place to stay? She frowned as she tried to remember if he had mentioned where he was staying.

"Did you…" she started, but she was interrupted by the older man.

"That should do it," he said, leaning back and dusting off his hands. "Give it a try now."

She pulled out her keys and sat behind the wheel. When her car turned on the first try, she closed her eyes and relaxed. "Thank you," she said to Reagan again.

"I'll take care of the bill," he told her.

"No, I can…" She stopped when he gave her a look that told her he wanted to pay for her.

He walked over and handed the man a twenty, when the guy tried to tell him it was fifty dollars, Reagan narrowed his eyes at him.

"Is that the price for almost screwing your customers

out of the fee of a tow for no reason?" he said calmly, and Clara was instantly grateful to have Reagan handling the men instead of dealing with them herself. She would have probably lost her temper and cried at the same time.

Reagan ignored the man's anger and turned away to walk back over to her.

"How about some breakfast?" she suggested. "It's the least I can do for all of your help." She watched out of the corner of her eye as the father- son duo drove away. "You just saved me my last hundred dollars, not to mention, I owe you for paying."

"I could eat." Reagan smiled. "How about Cowboy Kitchen?" he suggested. "It's just down the street."

"I love that place." She smiled.

"I'll follow you there," he suggested and shut her car door for her.

As she drove the block and a half to her favorite break-fast place, she was grateful she hadn't needed to walk back home. The sun was fully up now, and it was easily in the high eighties. When she'd walked to her car from her apartment, she'd worn a jacket to fend off the pre-summer chill in the air.

She had a few hours left before she was due back at work and had planned on spending some time at the beach after it had warmed up if she had managed to get her car fixed. Now, however, she wanted to spend her precious few hours with Reagan, trying to break through the rough exterior and find out all she could about the man. She knew it was probably going to end badly, but she was tired of hiding. After five years of being on her own, she figured a little enjoyment couldn't hurt.

hey ate breakfast out on the patio, watching the tourists rush around as if they were in a hurry to get somewhere to relax.

"Something tells me you're used to busy tourist spots," she said to him out of the blue.

He'd been watching a family walking down the pathway towards the beach. The father was pulling a small cart carrying two kids, beach towels, chairs, an umbrella, and a cooler probably loaded with enough food to last a week. The mother had a baby in her arms and another one in her large belly.

"Yeah," he said, finishing off his juice. "I grew up not far from here." He turned to her. "You?"

"California," she answered, figuring that since it was one of the biggest states, it was safe to give him a little detail of her past life.

"What brought you here?" he asked.

"Work," she said easily enough. It was true. She'd fled

that night so many years ago and had pinballed around the country from job to job, ending up at Rico's.

"I'm sure there are plenty of waitress jobs in California."

"I wanted to travel. To see the world." She avoided his gaze.

"How long have you been at Rico's?" he asked her, causing her eyes to return to him.

"A little over a year."

"So, are you done with seeing the world?" he asked her. She looked away again.

"For now, I'm happy where I am." She turned to him. "What about you? Your job must take you plenty of places."

"It has, yes," he answered her. He figured that if he gave her a little of his past, she might relax and open up some to him. "I spent a few years in the Special Forces. I traveled a lot back then," he admitted.

"What happened?" His eyebrows shot up in question. "I assume you are no longer with the Forces. Why did you get out?"

"Medical discharge." This caused her eyebrows to raise even more.

"You said that. I mean, were you shot?"

He nodded. "Took a bullet to the back and thigh." He rubbed the spot on his leg that still bothered him in cold weather.

"No wonder the scratch you received last night didn't faze you." She relaxed again. "Then what? You started... saving people for a living?"

He chuckled. "After a very difficult year of healing and learning to walk again, yes."

"It was that bad?"

He sobered. "I lost several of my comrades that day."

"I'm sorry," she said softly. "What made you decide to go into this line of work once you were healed?"

"It's what I was made to do." He leaned back and quickly ran through his past, telling her about how his mom had hidden him away to protect him. How his father had found them and saved them from the cult. Then, how he'd spent the rest of his life with the goal of helping others out of the same kind of horror he and his aunts and uncles had been through as children.

"So, every one of your aunts and uncles came from abusive homes?" she asked almost half an hour later. They had left the small diner and had slowly been walking along the beach together.

"Yeah," he answered. "My aunt Cassey was starved by her stepmother and beaten by her father. My uncle Marcus..." He thought of the horrors the rest of them had been through. "Well, let's just say they were all very lucky Lilly came along and rescued them. Mark and Elizabeth Grayton were heaven sent."

"It sounds like it. You're lucky to have such an amazing family." She glanced down at her watch. "I... need to get back home to shower before my shift starts." She glanced over her shoulder. "Are you still planning on coming in tonight?"

"Yeah." He nodded.

She leaned closer to him. "You might want to change shirts first." She touched his jacket. "I don't know how you can stand to be wearing this thing in this heat."

He'd forgotten about his jacket, or the fact that he hadn't had time to go back to his hotel room and shower or change, since he'd been dealing with the guy who had attacked her last night.

"Yeah, I…" What? He didn't want to tell her what had happened. "I will," he finished, and they started walking back towards their cars.

She stopped when they reached the end of the trail to the beach. "You do have a place to stay, right?"

"Yes." He chuckled. "I just didn't have time to change shirts."

"Why not?" she asked as they crossed the street and started walking towards the parking lot.

"I had… things to take care of after I left your place."

They stopped by her car. "Did it have anything to do with what happened last night?"

He thought about telling her but knew it wouldn't really do any good. Besides, he wanted an excuse to see her again tonight.

"No," he lied. The look on Clara's face told him that she wasn't buying it. "I better go." He turned away.

"You're still stopping by tonight?" she asked before he could get too far away.

"Yes, I'll be there," he assured her, noting her instant smile.

"I'll keep the beer chilled for you," she called after him. "And Rico on a leash."

He chose not to look back, but instead, jumped into the truck and drove back to his hotel. He showered and carefully shaved around the nick on his neck. Dressing in a fresh shirt and jeans, he pulled out his phone when it rang.

The call was from his aunt Julie. She had taken a trip to Arizona to visit his sister. Julie was letting him know that she was heading back home and that Bella, as everyone liked to call his sister Isabella, was doing fine.

He'd known that himself, since he called her on a weekly basis. Usually he got her voicemail, but when he did, his sister always texted or called him back.

After he hung up with his aunt, he called his mother. The phone was handed back and forth between his parents as they filled him in on their latest news. He mentioned to them that he might swing back home in a week or two after he was done with his current job, and they both grew excited and started making plans for a family gathering at his grandfather's home, the house his parents had been raised in together.

He glanced down at his watch and figured Clara had been on shift for almost an hour.

"I better get back to work." He shifted the phone and chuckled when he heard his mother sigh. "I'll call again when I can."

"Go," his mom said. "Save the world." This time he heard his father chuckle.

"Take care and be safe," his father said before hanging up.

He tucked his phone in his back pocket and made sure to strap his gun against his skin once more. He may have captured the man who had jumped him last night, but something told him there would be more. He hadn't gotten as far as he had by not knowing when to be cautious.

Pulling into the parking lot less than half an hour later, he stopped next to her older sedan and looked it over before heading inside.

He didn't have to request to be seated in her section, since it was free seating. Picking a booth that looked out over the water, he watched her from across the room. He knew the moment she realized that he was there. Her shoulders straightened before she glanced over her shoulder and locked eyes with him.

He'd planned to smile at her, but seeing her dark eyes meet his had his heart jumping in his chest. Damn. He was in real trouble.

She made her way across the room and stopped next to his table.

"Problem?" she asked, frowning down at him.

"No." He'd had time to relax and clear his mind before she got closer. "I'll have…"

"A beer?" she jumped in.

"I didn't eat yet, so add a burger and fries."

She wrote down his order and then glanced back up at him. "You looked worried."

"Just being cautious. See anyone stalking around?" He glanced around the restaurant.

"Just you." She smiled and turned to place his order. He watched her as much as he could without drawing too much attention to himself.

Rico glared at him from behind the bar, but since he didn't cross the room and kick his ass, he figured Clara had talked to him and filled him in on what had happened last night. Still, the man continued to watch him when he could.

By the time Clara returned with his food and beer, Rico was too busy to keep an eye on them.

"Sit for a moment." He motioned to the bench across from him. Her eyes moved to the bar area and, seeing that her boss was busy, she sat on the edge of the seat.

"Thanks for… well, everything," she said softly as her eyes continued to scan her tables for customers in need.

"It's what I do." He took a sip of his beer. "Have you thought any more on why someone would target you?" he asked, causing her eyes to zoom back to his. When her face turned pale, he realized he'd spooked her.

~

"Target?" She frowned and felt the blood drain from her head.

He leaned closer to her. "You do realize that whoever tried to jump you disabled your car first, right? Meaning…" He paused to let his words sink in. Her shoulders slumped as she leaned back in the booth as it sank in and hit home.

"They were after me. They knew it was my car." She closed her eyes. Her head started to spin, and she felt her breathing quicken.

"Hey." He rushed to her side, nudging her further into the booth so he would have room to sit beside her. "It's okay, I'm here—"

His words were cut off when he was yanked out of the booth. Clara watched in horror as Rico's meaty fist plowed into Reagan's chin, causing his head to snap back.

Then, to her surprise and horror, Reagan ducked the next punch and twisted around behind her boss. He held Rico's fists behind him as she jumped out of the booth and started to berate the older man.

"What did you do that for?" She got in his face. "Reagan was helping me." She lowered her voice as she shot looks around the room. The customers were all watching them. Some had even taken out their cell phones and were videoing them just in case something more exciting happened.

"He…" Rico swallowed and narrowed his eyes at her. "He shoved you in the booth and you looked like you were about to throw up."

She knew that her boss had just been trying to protect her. She laid a hand on his arm to comfort him.

"He was coming over to comfort me, after…" Her eyes moved to Reagan's for help in explaining.

"Clara was upset about…" She could tell that he was trying to think of an excuse quickly, but nothing was coming to mind.

"A bad tip," she threw out, feeling stupid once the words were out. She decided to redirect the man instead of explaining further. "Really, Rico, Reagan was just trying to make me feel better."

She noticed that Rico had finally relaxed in Reagan's arms. Reagan dropped his hold on him and took a giant step away from him. No doubt, just in case.

"You're okay?" Rico asked her.

"Yes." She smiled up at her boss. "He's helping me. Honest," she said softly.

"Well, shit." Rico sighed and turned to Reagan. "I'm… sorry." Rico looked like he'd swallowed something foul as he apologized. She wanted to laugh, but held it in.

Reagan wiggled his jaw. "No harm."

That caused her boss to chuckle. "Right, I've got a right hook like a sledge…" He stopped when she cleared her throat and crossed her arms over her chest.

"We are not going to start comparing body parts, are we?" she asked dryly.

Rico chuckled. "You must have a jaw of steel."

"I've been told that before," Reagan said easily before sobering and adding, "I'm glad Clara has a boss like you to look out for her." He shook the man's outstretched hand.

"Your dinner is on the house." Rico motioned to Reagan's burger and drink before turning around and heading back to the bar.

"I'm sorry," she said.

"Don't be. If he had been there last night, I'm sure you wouldn't have been jumped." He motioned for her to slide into the booth again, then sat on his side once more.

"Are you okay?" she asked, seeing a small bruise form under the bigger one from last night.

"Yeah." He touched his jaw, then picked up his beer. "Nothing a cold beer and a free meal can't solve," he joked, but his eyes remained on her. "How about you?"

CHAPTER 5

*H*ow was she? Clara thought to herself as she finished her shift. She'd blown Reagan off earlier when he'd asked her, since she hadn't technically been on break and her customers needed attention.

Thankfully, she'd been able to avoid chatting with him any more during her shift, since a large group of tourists had arrived after that.

Now, it was only half an hour until closing and the place was emptying out. Reagan hadn't moved from his spot, except to step outside for a phone call.

Since he'd mentioned that whoever had attacked her last night had come specifically for her, she'd found it hard to focus.

The fact was, she knew exactly what she needed to do. She needed to pack up and leave. Tell Rico she was moving on, give notice at her apartment, and disappear again.

She'd planned where she'd go next, shortly after she'd arrived in town almost a year ago. She found it better to think things through earlier on rather than at the last moment.

She even had a bug-out bag packed in the bottom of her closet. One which she had hoped she wouldn't ever have to use. Now, she was thinking about the long drive that she was going to have to make that night. There was no time like the present. If the guy that had attacked her was still around, there was nothing stopping him from coming back tonight or the next day. She was living on borrowed time.

"Are you okay?" Rico asked her once she closed out her account for the night.

She leaned on the counter and felt her eyes sting. "I… Rico, I… need a break." She bit her bottom lip to stop herself from crying.

His eyes ran over her. "Sure thing, baby girl. Take a few days…" She shook her head, stopping him.

"I need longer than that." Her eyes moved past him and landed on the back of Reagan's head. "It might be best if you look for another waitress."

Rico's hand rested on her arm. "This isn't about today… I told you, I thought he was—"

"No." She straightened. "It has nothing to do with Reagan." After all, that was the truth, right? Reagan wasn't what had spooked her.

"Then what?" Rico asked.

"I just… need to go home," she lied.

Rico stared at her for a moment. "To Texas?"

She'd forgotten she'd told him she'd come from Dallas. It was partially true. She'd been in Dallas for a few months prior to coming here.

"Yeah." She nodded and took a deep breath.

"When are you going?" he asked, but she could see the fear in his eyes.

"Tonight." She avoided his eyes.

When he was silent, she glanced over at him. The frown on his face and the sad look in his eyes told her everything.

No matter what happened, she couldn't risk Rico getting hurt. The scene from last night had played over in her mind. What if, instead of Reagan stepping out to save her, Rico had been there, and the bullet hadn't just grazed his neck. She didn't want anything bad to happen to the man who had looked out for her more than her father ever had.

"Rico, it may just be for a while." She touched his arm again. "I'll let you know, after I get there."

He sighed and shocked her by gathering her up in his arms. "Be safe," he said and then kissed the top of her head. "You've always got a place here if you need one."

"Thanks," she said, holding in the tears again.

She doubted she could explain to Reagan why she was crying when he walked her out to her car. Something in her gut told her that if she explained to Reagan that she had to leave, he would talk her out of going.

"You'd better go," Rico said, dropping his arms from around her. "Your new friend looks like he's about ready to storm over here and pay me back for the right hook I gave him earlier."

She glanced over and sure enough, Reagan was watching them. Closely.

She pulled away. "I'd better go."

"Don't be a stranger. I expect to hear that you made it home okay," he said to her. "Stay safe."

"I will," she said, wishing she could rush across the bar again and hug him one more time. Instead, she grabbed her purse from behind the counter and walked over to where Reagan was waiting for her.

"What was that all about?" he asked softly when they stepped out into the dark parking lot.

"Rico was just apologizing to me one more time about the scene he made," she lied, avoiding his eyes. "Do you think it's safe?" she asked, changing the subject.

"For now." He turned his attention to the darkness.

She could feel him go from relaxed to tense quickly.

"What?" she asked, just before he pushed her to the ground. Loud popping sounds exploded around them.

She felt part of the wood doors rain down on them, sending shards of glass and wood into her hair and hands as she covered her face, the only part of her body that hadn't been covered by Reagan's large form.

"Stay put," he growled when the night turned silent again.

She couldn't have moved if she needed to. She was frozen on the sidewalk as his heavy body disappeared from her own.

"What the…" Rico shouted as he rushed to her side. "Are you hurt, baby girl?" he asked her, sitting her up and scanning her for injuries.

"I… I'm…" She bit her bottom lip, but it was too late. This time, the dam holding back her feelings exploded as Rico wrapped her in his arms for a second time that night.

Reagan ran across the parking lot towards the area where

he'd seen the dark figure. Luckily, he'd seen the outline of the man and had been able to get Clara down before the shots rang out.

He hated leaving her there on the ground, but he wanted to get some information from this guy, since the last one wouldn't talk. He'd spent all night with the man he'd caught earlier, and the guy wouldn't tell him or the local police anything.

Maybe this guy would.

But by the time he got to where he'd seen the figure, the only thing remaining were empty bullet casings.

"Shit." He sighed and tucked his gun back into his holster.

When he turned around, he was shocked to see Clara's taillights disappearing out of the parking lot.

He rushed back to where Rico stood. Watching her drive away, he asked, "Where is she going?"

"Dallas." Rico shook his head. "Tell me that someone didn't just shoot at her."

He growled instead of answering and rushed to his truck.

"You'd better protect my girl," Rico called out.

"That's what I'm trying to do." He peeled out of the parking lot.

When he parked behind her car, blocking her in, he relaxed a little knowing she couldn't get around him this time.

"What do you think you were doing?" he asked her a few minutes later. He'd leaned against the railing just outside her front door and waited for her, his arms crossed over his chest as he tried to get his breathing and heart rate back to normal. She'd almost been killed. And it would have been his fault for being focused on her instead of her safety.

Clara squealed and dropped a huge overnight bag as she spun around to face him. Her hand covered her heart as she glared at him.

"I'm leaving," she said when she recovered. She bent to pick up the bag, but he was faster.

She must have packed everything she owned in the thing. It was almost heavier than she was.

"Going…?" He let his question hang in the air.

"Anywhere but here," she said quickly as she reached for her bag. He held it out of her reach.

"Good, then you won't mind if we swing by my hotel room to get my things first." He tossed the bag over his shoulders and started walking towards his truck.

She rushed to catch up with him. "I'm not… going with you," she finished at the bottom of the stairs.

He was too busy scanning the parking lot to give her any attention as he tossed her bag in the back of his truck.

"What are you…" She reached for the bag.

"Will your car be okay here?" he asked, holding the door open for her.

"No." She frowned. "I'm driving it away." She again reached for her bag, but he stepped in front of her.

"Listen, before you decide to leave your life and everyone that loves you here, come stay with me for a while, at least for a few nights. I'm sure we can figure this out. After all, it is what I do. Remember?" he said softly, touching her shoulders. "Please, let me help."

He knew the moment she changed her mind. He could see the weariness in her eyes almost consume her.

"Just for a few days," she said, and he helped her up into the truck.

When he got in beside her, she turned to him. "Where are we going?"

"First things first, will your car be okay here for a while?"

She glanced out the window and nodded. "It's my assigned spot. Until I give Mrs. Johnson notice, I'm allowed to park there."

"Good." He pulled out of the parking lot and started heading home. "My family lives about an hour from here." He glanced over at her. "I promised my mom and aunt a visit." He smiled. "You're going to like them."

He could feel her tension across the darkness. "It's not like that," he added. "You needed a place, a safe place to be." He shrugged. "Home is the safest place I know."

CHAPTER 6

*C*lara must have fallen asleep shortly after they stopped to get his things from his hotel room. When the truck finally came to a stop, she was jolted awake, forgetful of where she was and what was happening. Then, suddenly, it all came back to her, and she found herself more tired than before.

"We're here," Reagan said cheerfully as he glanced out the front window.

A massive house sat in front of them. Almost every light was on in the place, illuminating it like a lighthouse. Its white paint gleamed in the truck's headlights. There were black shutters on the windows and several brick chimney stacks rose up from the roof. But it was the massive front porch that made the older home charming. It wrapped around both sides of the home, as if embracing it.

"This is home?" she asked, taking in the multiple swings and chairs on the porch, which made the place looked lived in and loved. Potted plants lined each porch step. There were several bird baths, and feeders hung on the corner of the deck area.

"It was once," he agreed. "Come on in. I called ahead to let them know we were coming." He jumped out and rushed around to open her door, then reached in for her bag.

She followed him up the stairs, admiring the blooming plants. Once, she'd enjoyed helping her mother work in the flower garden. Long ago. Sadness threatened to surface so she turned away as Reagan opened the front door without even knocking.

"We're here," he called out as he set their bags by the front door. Several dogs came rushing towards them. Both large, droopy-looking hounds let out barks, but then Reagan bent down and started giving them attention. They practically jumped into his arms, then rolled on the ground, exposing their bellies while their tongues fell out of their mouths.

"This is Chase," he said looking up at her, "and that one is Catch." He nodded to the other dog. "Brothers." He laughed when they almost knocked him over. "Okay, go on now." He snapped his fingers, which had the dogs disappearing into the house. "My grandfather says he started collecting dogs when he couldn't keep up with kids anymore." He chuckled as he stood back up. "Mom?" he called out. "Dad?" he said loudly again.

"They might be asleep," she said in hushed tones.

"No, they live down the street. Just my granddad lives here now with the mutts. They must be out back." He motioned for her to follow him through the house.

She admired the gleaming hardwood floors and modern furniture as they passed through the house quickly.

"We're here," he called out again as they stepped out of the back screen door.

"There you are." A blonde woman jumped up from a chair arranged around a stone firepit, a glass of wine in her hands. She rushed over to Reagan and hugged him. The two men were slower to come join her.

The younger man pulled Reagan into his arms and hugged him. Even though Reagan overshadowed the man in height, Clara could tell instantly that this was his father.

The older man was then gathered into Reagan's lighter embrace. "How are you doing, Granddad?"

"I'm still kicking," the man joked, patting his arm. "Who have you brought to us then?"

"Everyone, this is Clara. Clara, my family," Regan answered.

After quick introductions were made, she was handed a glass of wine and shuffled into a chair around the warm firepit.

"Are you hungry?" Reagan's mother, Marissa, asked as soon they sat down.

"You know me, I can always eat," Reagan joked. He took the beer his father offered.

"I've got some chicken I can reheat." His grandfather jumped in. He started to get up, but Roman, Reagan's father, put his hand on the older man's shoulder to keep him in his chair.

"I'll get it, Dad," he said easily and disappeared into the house.

"So, Clara, I've promised my son that I won't ask too many questions." Marissa smiled across the fire at her. "I understand this is a... work thing?"

"Yes," Clara jumped in quickly to confirm. She didn't

want his family to think that he was bringing her home to get their approval. She'd dreamed of having a normal life at one point in her life, but it was no longer a possibility.

"Okay, I'll keep my nagging mother questions to a minimum then," Marissa joked as she sipped her own wine. Then her eyes locked with Clara's. "Where are you from, Clara?" she asked.

Seeing no reason to lie to Reagan's family, she answered.

"California originally." She sipped her own wine and relaxed back in the chair, enjoying the warmth of the firepit.

"Did you go to school?"

"Some," she admitted. She thought of her last day at college.

"Didn't like it?" Reagan's grandfather asked.

"No, I loved it," she admitted. "Very much, but…" She thought of the reason she hadn't been able to return to classes and frowned. "I needed to move on."

"Reagan loved it as well, so we were a little surprised when he joined the military. Still, it suited him. So does what he does now." She smiled at her son.

"Ever since I met the kid," his grandfather started, "rescuing strays was all he could think about." The man scratched the dog's head as it leaned on his knee. "He found these two in a bag tossed on the side of the high-way." He nodded to the dogs.

"They weren't the first or the last, either," his mother added with a smile.

"He's our very own Saint Jude." His grandfather chuckled.

Is that why he was helping her? Because it was just in

his nature? Maybe the sexual tension she'd been feeling was one sided? But what about that kiss?

Her head was starting to swim from the lack of food and weariness brought on by the past twenty-four hours.

"You look tired," Reagan mentioned, getting her attention.

Sighing, she nodded. "I am."

"Food's warmed up," his father called out to them.

"We'll let you head in then." Marissa stood up. "It's about time we got home ourselves. Dad, we'll be by tomorrow to install those new bushes." She turned to her father.

"Coming in, Granddad?" Reagan asked.

"No, I'm going to sit out here for a little longer. You know where everything is." He turned to her. "While you're here, my home is your home. Please, help yourself. If you need anything… just let me know."

"Thank you." She stood up and looked at the faces of his family. "All of you." She followed Reagan inside, past his parents as they said their own goodbyes.

She'd been expecting warmed fried chicken, but what was waiting for them was a full kitchen of food. Grilled chicken breasts in lemon sauce, a huge pan of mashed potatoes with gravy, and spring vegetables.

"If we're lucky…" Reagan started and then smiled as he stuck his head in the fridge. "Yup, chocolate cake for dessert. Let's dig in." He handed her a plate.

After showing Clara the guest bedroom and bathroom, he

disappeared into his old bedroom down the hallway, pulled out his laptop, and got to work.

After contacting his client and telling him he'd hit a snag, he did a little more research on her family and her past.

What should have been a simple cut-and-dried case of her sister's murder still didn't sit right in his mind. The police had marked the case unsolved but hadn't been pursuing Clara, even though she was still their main suspect.

Her taking off could be seen as an admission of guilt, yet after watching her for a few days, he began to doubt it. She seemed more scared than guilty. But scared of what?

Her father, Carlo Cruz, had built up his real estate company, Sunset Dreams Realty, from virtually nothing. He'd bought a defunct shopping center for less than a hundred-grand, tore it down, and built a couple of high-rise apartment complexes. Within several years, he was a multi-millionaire.

Several years later, he married his high school sweetheart and had two daughters, Clara and Gina. When Clara was seven, her mother died from a mysterious illness. Carlo remained single for a few years, but shortly after Clara's tenth birthday, he remarried the girl's nanny, Rebecca.

There were news articles and pictures of Clara being taken into police custody in her blue party dress the evening of her sister's murder. Confusion marred her face and when he found an image that he could zoom in on, he noticed her eyes were unfocused and red from tears. There was blood splattered all over her dress and her arms, which police confirm came from her sister. But, since she hadn't had a scratch on her and there hadn't been any solid evidence, Clara had never officially been charged.

Her father had stepped out of public view since his youngest daughter's death, apparently trying to run his business from the privacy of his massive modern-looking home in the Hollywood Hills.

There were several articles on the home prominently featuring Carlo's new wife, Rebecca. The woman seemed to love the spotlight that her newfound wealth afforded her.

When his vision started blurring, he crawled into his bed and clocked out for a few hours. When he woke, it was to the dogs barking with excitement. The sun was streaming through the lace window curtains, and he realized he'd gotten more than just a few hours of sleep.

Showering quickly, he dressed and headed downstairs. When he found Clara sitting at the countertop watching his grandfather cook French toast with the dogs happily lying at his feet, he relaxed.

He hadn't really thought she would bail on him, but still, he'd worried.

"Morning," he said, getting their attention.

"Morning," they both said back to him.

Clara was smiling, as if she'd been enjoying the conversation.

"Your grandfather was telling me stories of you as a child." She rotated the barstool towards him. "How you didn't come here until you were seven…"

He nodded. "Yeah, I had no clue I even had a family, other than my mother, of course."

"So your grandfather was telling me. It's a fascinating

story, how you and your father were kidnapped by the cult your biological grandfather ran."

He swallowed hard, remembering the day so many years ago his father had risked everything to save him. "Yeah, Dad was shot as we escaped." He smiled suddenly. "And later, my mom kicked my BG's butt." He sat next to her and leaned closer. "That's what I call my biological grandfather, BG."

"Gave him a killer right hook. Just like I taught her," his father said from the doorway.

"Mom still says it was Aunt Cassey that taught her how to box," he joked, causing his father to chuckle.

"I taught both of them," he answered easily. "Dad, we've got those new bushes in already. When are the guys with the pine straw going to be here?"

"So quick?" His grandfather shook his head. "Not until noon. Why don't you two come on in and have some breakfast. I made plenty."

"Missy's taking the dogs for a quick walk and will be back soon. I'm starving." His dad sat on the other side of Clara. "Did you sleep well?" he asked her.

"Yes, thank you," she replied. He could tell she had; the worry in her eyes had disappeared. Her dark hair was still wet from the shower, and she looked very cozy with her feet tucked under her in the chair.

For the first time since he'd met her, she looked relaxed. His family had a knack for making people feel comfortable. It was one of the reasons he loved them so much and why he'd brought her here instead of taking her back to her own family.

CHAPTER 7

*A*fter eating a stack of French toast and several slices of bacon, Reagan suggested a walk down to the pond that sat behind the house. His mother had returned from her walk, and both of the dogs tagged along as they made their way down a worn pathway to the water's edge.

There was a small dock that hung over the calm water and had two large chairs at the end of it.

"Want to sit for a moment?" he asked her, motioning to the chairs.

"Sure." She relaxed in the chair and could just imagine spending the rest of the day in the sun, watching the dragonflies buzz around the water.

"This place is… amazing." She couldn't come up with a description good enough to match the place.

"Thanks." He glanced over at her. "Have you thought any further about… things?" he asked after a moment of silence passed between them.

Her entire body tensed once more as her mind jumped

to all of the possibilities she'd come up with. All of the ones she'd admit to herself but keep from him.

"I have," she answered. "I'm thinking I was a thief's mark." She could tell instantly that he didn't agree with her assessment. "I've heard of that sort of thing happening to other people in popular tourist spots."

"Usually to wealthy tourists." His dark eyebrows rose. "You are neither."

Her shoulders sank. "No, you're right."

"Any other ideas?"

"It could have been sexual," she said in a tiny voice. She hated mentioning this idea, since she knew what it likely really was, but she couldn't very well blurt that one out to him. Reagan didn't know about her past.

"It could have been, but people don't usually shoot at someone for sexual reasons," he said as he looked out over the water.

She turned and watched a pair of ducks swimming towards them.

"Maybe it is someone from your past... you know, before you started moving around?" he suggested.

She bit her bottom lip, desperately wanting to share her history with him but afraid of how it would change his mind about her.

After all, it was a big turn off to find out that someone you had invited into your family's home had been accused of murdering her own sister.

"No," she lied as she avoided looking in his direction. "Like I said before, no one from my past is looking for me."

The silence stretched on until he turned to her a few minutes later.

"Clara, I haven't been completely honest with you." Just then, both of the dogs barked happily and rushed off the dock, heading back towards the house.

They both turned around and saw his father walking towards them.

"Sorry to bother you two, but I was hoping to enlist my son in digging up a few bushes and moving them."

Something told her that Reagan was thankful for the interruption.

"Sure." He stood up and looked down at her. "You're welcome to enjoy." He nodded to the lake.

She thought about it and stood with him. "Actually, if it's okay with you, I'd rather help." Upon his look, she shrugged. "It's been a while since I worked outside. I enjoy it."

"Suit yourself." He motioned for her to lead the way.

For the next hour, she dug in the dirt, planting flowers around the back porch, adding new rose bushes to around the firepit. They planted a few purple wisteria plants, some pink azaleas, and a live oak in the side yard.

It had been too long since she'd had her hands in the dirt. She lost herself in the simple pleasure and didn't notice her back and arms hurting from the exhaustion.

They broke for lunch, and Reagan's grandfather and mother brought out a tray full of turkey sandwiches and homemade French fry crisps.

After lunch, Reagan and his father pulled up some dead bushes along the garage. Both men had pulled off their shirts while they worked and were coated in sweat as they dug and chopped the old roots away from the foundation.

She noticed a small flower bed full of weeds and sat

down in the grass to free the growing flowers from them. Again, she lost herself in the work and her own thoughts. She tried not to glance over at Reagan and watch him work with his shirt off, but he was so sexy that she found it hard not to enjoy the way the sun danced across his muscles.

She kept telling herself that he was just being kind to her because it's what he did. After all, his family had made a point to mention it. She'd hoped that he felt the same way about her as she did about him, but it was starting to look more and more like he didn't.

"You're pretty good at this sort of thing," a deep voice said from above her. Glancing up, she tried to smile at Reagan.

"I used to work in the yard with my mother," she said before really thinking. She'd been open and truthful with him and his family and hadn't really seen any reason not to be, but there were some things she still wanted to keep to herself.

She watched his eyebrows go up. "Oh?" He frowned. "Used to?" he asked, sitting on the upturned bucket next to her.

"She died when I was seven." She dusted off her hands.

"I'm sorry," he said softly and touched her arm.

"I only remember a handful of things about her." She leaned back on her heels and closed her eyes as memories played in her brain. "Working in the garden, playing in the water at the beach." She smiled and opened her eyes and looked around. "But it's the gardening I remember the most. It was our time. The beach was family time. I think Gina enjoyed the beach more."

"Gina?" he asked, and she felt her heart sink. She'd

said too much. Allowed her guard to go down. Fear spiked deep in her gut and she fought for her next words.

"My sister," Clara finally answered.

He could see the inner battle as she fought to come up with the words.

"Something tells me she's not with you anymore?" he asked, feeling dirty for already knowing the answer. He'd been ready to tell her everything at the lake. But now, he was questioning telling her. After all, he had to figure out how to convince her to go with him back to California when they were done here.

"She died a few years back."

"I'm sorry," he said again, this time keeping his hands to himself. She'd relaxed back on the grass.

"What about your father?" he asked, hoping she would keep opening up to him. The more she talked, the surer he was of her innocence.

Her eyes moved up to his. "He's alive still." She shrugged. "He's back in California with his new wife."

The tone in her voice told him more than all the research had last night. "You don't like her?" he asked.

She flipped a strand of her hair away from her eyes. "She's okay. She was our nanny before…"

"Now she's married to him," he added as if he understood. "That must have been difficult."

"No, not really. She was always nice to both of us. Even after they married, she was kind."

"But…" He let the question hang in the air.

"It just wasn't the same after. Dad wasn't the same."

She leaned forward and pulled at another weed. "Then Gina died and… I moved away."

"How about another walk?" he suggested, standing up. "We can cool off in the pond, if you want," he added.

"I've never swum in a pond before." She glanced around. "Aren't there alligators in Florida?"

He chuckled. "Yes, but the little ones in the pond are about the size of my arm." He watched fear jump into her eyes and laughed even harder. "Trust me, they're more afraid of you than the other way around.

"I seriously doubt that," she said, allowing him to pull her to her feet.

"You swim in the ocean… think of all the sharks in those waters. Besides, I'll be right there, protecting you from the gators."

Her eyes narrowed. "Who's going to protect you?"

He started walking towards the lake as he wrapped his arm around her shoulders. "You can," he joked.

He wasn't surprised when the dogs followed them once more.

When they reached the dock, he pulled his shirt, jeans, and shoes off and rushed off the end of the dock, both dogs on his heels as they splashed into the cool water.

It was early enough in spring that the water hadn't warmed up much yet. The chilly water instantly refreshed him.

"Come on in," he said, laughing as the dogs swam in circles around him. "The water's perfect." She glanced around slowly. "Trust me, whatever you have, it's been seen plenty of times here. Almost everyone in my family has jumped into the lake at one point in nothing but their underwear."

"It's not that…" She crossed her arms over her chest. "I was looking for those arm-length gators you were talking about."

He laughed again. "The dogs probably scared them off." He motioned for her to join him.

He had expected to enjoy the view of her standing at the end of the dock in her underwear, but he hadn't anticipated that seeing her like that would be like a punch to the gut. She was even more beautiful than he'd imagined in her simple cream-colored bra-and-panty set.

She jumped into the water so quickly, he only got a quick glimpse. Still, it was enough that he was pretty sure he'd be thinking about her like that every time he saw her.

When she surfaced, her hair was pushed away from her face. She gasped.

"It's freezing." She kicked her feet and moved her arms to stay afloat.

He laughed. "It's refreshing." He smiled. "In another month it will be too hot to cool off in."

"I'd rather be too hot than frozen at the bottom of a lake." She started making her way to the shore, but he stopped her by grabbing her arm and tugging her body next to his.

Her hands went to his shoulders as they kicked to keep their heads above the water.

"There, you can have some of my body heat," he said softly as he looked down at her face.

He felt her suck in her breath as she watched his lips. His eyes moved to her lips, and he once again wished to taste them.

"Why are you doing this?" she asked, just under her breath.

"I would have thought that it was obvious by now," he said truthfully, his eyes moving to her darker ones. "You feel so good next to me. So soft." He rubbed his hands up her sides, enjoying the feeling of her silky skin in his hands.

When he pulled her closer, she gripped him harder and allowed him to hold them upright in the water.

"Clara, I really want to kiss you again," he said when she didn't speak. But before he could bend his head down to hers, she moved up and laid her lips over his.

She tasted even better than before. Maybe it was because her almost naked body was glued to his, or maybe it was because she'd opened up to him more. Either way, he found it hard to concentrate on not drowning as she slanted her lips and opened for him.

"My god," he said softly next to her skin. He didn't know why he was breathing so hard. He'd spent the last hour cutting out six massive evergreen bushes, roots and all, and hadn't felt this winded. "We'd better move to shallower ground before we drown," he joked. He started kicking them towards the sandy shore while he held onto her.

"You have a beach," she said, glancing over his shoulder.

"Yeah, my dad and my uncles and I trucked in the sand ourselves." He smiled. "Best summer of my life." He felt the soft sand under his feet and pulled her closer. Giving her no time to recover, he took her lips again. This time he was able to explore her body a little more with his hands. He ran them up and down her sides, over her soft butt, pulling her closer to him. She moaned when she felt him hard and ready against her.

When he realized he could take her right there, he forced his hold on her to loosen. There were too many lies between them.

He'd never mixed work with pleasure before. He'd never wanted to, until her.

CHAPTER 8

Clara wrapped her legs around Reagan and held on as her body vibrated and demanded more. She needed him to touch her, needed to feel his heated skin against her own. Wanted more than anything to allow herself to let go, just for one moment. Just this time.

But then the dogs rushed over to them, splashing water on them, and she chuckled and pulled away from Reagan.

Reagan easily let her go, shielding her from most of the water sprinkles from the wet dogs.

"Sorry, they have no manners." One of the dogs rushed up to him and started climbing on his shoulders. "Or sense of personal space," he added with a laugh as he picked up the dog easily. He tossed it playfully into the water. The other dog, seeing what fun its brother was having, rushed over to do the same.

She could tell that it was something he'd done before, lifting the massive dogs in his powerful arms and tossing them across the pond as if they weighed no more than a pebble.

She laughed and enjoyed watching the game until the dogs tired of it and disappeared into the tall grass surrounding the pond. Then Reagan returned to her side once more.

She felt her heart skip. But then she was screaming as he picked her up and, much like he'd done with the dogs, tossed her high up into the air. For one split second, she was weightless and carefree as she flew over the calm water. Then she landed in the water with a splash and sank below the surface. Instead of coming up for air, she swam towards him under the dark surface until she felt his legs and tugged playfully on his shorts.

She heard him laugh and he reached for her, but she twisted and kicked away from him, keeping out of his reach.

When her shoulder brushed against something massive and scaly, she rushed towards the sandy shore as fast as she could. Surfacing, she sputtered water out as she rushed to get out of the water, as images of a massive alligator rushing after her filled her mind.

"A gator," she cried out, her eyes scanning the water quickly. "Hurry, get out." She waved at Reagan and called out to him from the dry shore.

Reagan stood waist deep in the water, laughing at her.

"It was a fish," he finally said when he was done laughing. "About this big." He held his hands apart. "Trust me, I've been trying to catch old red for years." He laughed some more.

"Are you sure?" she asked, unwilling to stick a toe in the water now that she'd felt something slimy in there.

He chuckled and walked towards her, and she forgot everything except the gorgeous man heading her way. It reminded her of the scene in the James Bond movie Casino Royale where Daniel Craig walked out of the water. Damn, she was in trouble.

How was she supposed to keep her distance with someone like Reagan?

He didn't stop walking until their bodies were right up against one another's again.

"Clara, I... I want you, but there's something I need to clear up first."

"Okay," she said a little breathless.

His eyes moved around and then he sighed. "Let's go sit down." He nodded to a couple lawn chairs sitting in the grass a few feet away. "We can dry out and talk."

She followed him and sat down, enjoying the way the sun warmed her. Only when she looked down at herself did she realize that her bra and panties were completely see through, thanks to the water.

But Reagan didn't seem to notice now. He was watching the water as if he was trying to come up with the right words.

"Remember how I said... what I do for a living?" he started, keeping his eyes straight ahead.

"Yes," she said slowly. "You help people."

"Right." He took a deep breath. "I was hired by..." He turned to her now, his eyes locking with her own. "I was hired by your family to find you," he said quickly.

She stilled. Her breath locked in her lungs as his words sank in. When she felt her vision gray, she sucked in a deep breath and closed her eyes as she focused on breathing normally.

"Your dad and stepmother hired me to find you," he said, reaching for her hand, but she yanked it away and stood quickly. When she felt her world spin, she held onto the back of the chair.

"You're just now getting around to telling me this?" she ground out.

"I should have told you that first night," he admitted, standing beside her as he held his hands out towards her. "I should have said something before I kissed you."

She gripped the back of the chair until her knuckles turned white.

"You were there, at Rico's, because of me?" she asked. When he nodded, his eyes still on hers, she took a step backwards. "Did you… tell them where I was?" she asked.

"No, not yet."

"Why?" She shook her head. "Why not?"

"Because I… saw something different in you. I've been in the business of helping people too long not to know that where there are inconsistencies… there's usually trouble. I was right too. Someone else is after you. I'm pretty sure I was used." She saw his jaw flinch and knew he was holding in his anger.

Her mind whirled. She was just a job to him. He'd been paid to find her. Nothing more. He'd toyed with her from the first night he'd walked into Rico's place.

Taking another step back, she shook her head when he opened his mouth to talk. "I… need some time to think," she said quickly. She rushed over and gathered her clothes and sprinted down the path towards the house.

She was thankful when she was able to enter the house and rush up to the room where she'd spent last night in unseen.

Tossing her clothes down, she sat on the edge of the bed and closed her eyes as she ran over the past few days.

Tears threatened to escape her eyes, so she stood up and walked into the bathroom, pulled off her soaked underwear, and stepped into a warm shower. No matter how much she turned up the heat, she just couldn't get warm enough. Wrapping her arms around herself, she cried as she rested her forehead against the tile.

It was only a matter of time before she'd have to face the music. She could run again, she thought, and then quickly dismissed the idea. She was tired of running.

Sliding down the tile wall, she sat on the floor of the shower and hugged her knees to her chest as the water washed away her last hopes of freedom.

When Reagan entered the house, he could hear the shower running upstairs and pulled a beer from the fridge.

"What did you do now?" His grandfather was sitting in his rocking chair, a book in his lap. He moved into the living room and sat across from the old man.

He was pretty sure the old man hadn't aged a day since he'd first seen him twenty years ago. Which would be saying something if he hadn't looked as old as the hills to begin with. Still, it was hard to see any additional aging on the man who had come to mean so much to him and his family.

"I… told her that her family was looking for her. That they hired me to find her." His shoulders slumped.

"I always knew you were a terrible charmer." His grandfather chuckled as he shook his head.

"Hey now." He smiled quickly. "I get it honestly from you."

The old man laughed and set his book down, then leaned forward, his elbows resting on his knees. "There's a time to tell the truth and then there's a time not to."

"You think I should have lied to her?" he asked, a little shocked.

"Hell no." He chuckled. "I think you should have been honest with her from the beginning. But what's done is done. It's what happens next that matters." His grandfather leaned back and took a deep breath. "Did I ever tell you the story of how I met my Elizabeth?"

He thought about it and then shook his head. "No," he answered.

"It was back in my FBI days..." Reagan was so shocked he spit out the sip of beer he'd drunk.

"Holy shit, you were FBI?" he asked, his eyes running over the old man as if seeing him for the first time.

His grandfather smiled and nodded once again. "Sure was, for almost two decades." He leaned back and crossed his arms over his chest, his eyes going unfocused. "Your grandmother was my last assignment." He glanced up at the ceiling as if disappearing into his memories. "Elizabeth was the daughter of a senator. We got word that a political group had targeted several family members." His eyes returned to Reagan's. "They killed off four family members of other senators, all supposedly voting against a controversial bill."

"You were assigned to protect her?" he asked, curious, as his imagination took over.

"Yes." He sighed. "I failed." He frowned.

"What?" Reagan leaned forward. "But..."

"Your grandmother was shot." He closed his eyes as if reliving the horrible day. "The bullet went through the middle of her back, almost paralyzed her." He leaned over and picked up an old picture of the two of them in their younger days. Reagan had seen the photo all of his life, that and other ones from when his grandmother had been close to three hundred pounds. Still, his grandfather had always looked at the woman as if the sun rose and set just for her. "It limited her movement and when Karen and Julie were born, there were enough complications that it took away the ability for us to have more children. Because of the internal injuries and the babies shifting things around inside her, they nearly killed her when they were born. My Elizabeth had always wanted a dozen kids." His smile had returned. "I would have given her anything."

"You retired after..." He let the question hang in the air.

"Yes." He sighed. "Cashed out my pension, bought and traded some stocks in my friend's company and..." He shrugged. "Moved back home here, where I grew up, and rescued a few broken kids." He chuckled. "Had a blast seeing them grow up into strong men and women." He winked at him, something his grandfather did often.

Reagan's eyes moved to the ceiling when he heard the water turn off.

"There's something about this one," his grandfather said easily. "You've never brought home a woman, especially one that's *work*." His grandfather air quoted the last word, and Reagan chuckled.

"Clara is more than work," he admitted.

"I'm not blind." His grandfather laughed. "Well..." He stood up and groaned when his back cracked. "I promised your uncle Marcus I'd meet him and Shelly for dinner.

Rose is back in town for the weekend, and I've suddenly decided to spend the night with a beach view."

His uncle and aunt lived in the same house they purchased shortly after they'd met. The place looked over the Gulf of Mexico. He'd spent many nights himself in one of their guest rooms.

"Thanks." He stood up and hugged the fragile man. "I love you," he said as he held on.

"You are a pure joy. Your grandmother would be proud of you, as much as I am." His grandfather's wrinkled hand reached up and tapped him gently on the chin. "There's plenty of food in the ice box. Now, go smooth things over with your woman."

He chuckled as the old man pulled out his car keys and disappeared out the front door, whistling for the dogs to follow him. He stood inside the screen door and watched the dogs jump into the passenger side of the old truck. His grandfather drove off down the driveway.

"Was that your grandfather?" Clara asked from behind him.

He turned and then swallowed whatever he'd been about to say when he saw her standing in worn bleached shorts and a white tank top that clung to her curves. Her dark hair hung straight, still dripping from the shower.

The sun was setting, and bright hues of pink and yellows were streaming through the windows, playing over her skin and hair, making her skin almost glow. He'd never seen anything more beautiful. He didn't know what was going to happen in the next few days, but he was pretty sure that even if he had a lifetime to be with her, it wouldn't be nearly long enough.

CHAPTER 9

Clara watched Reagan move towards her. His eyes heated with desire, which caused her own body to react. She'd cried herself out in the shower and felt stupid for allowing her emotions to reign.

Now it was something else that controlled her—her desire for Reagan, to be touched again, to be wanted as much as he wanted her. It had been too long since she'd felt something like this.

Without a word, he pulled her into his arms and kissed her until her knees felt like jelly. Then his arms wrapped tightly around her, and he picked her up. She felt her world spin as he moved around the room.

When he bent her down, her eyes opened, and she realized he was laying her down on the sofa in the front room.

"Easy, we're alone," he said against her skin. "I just need… this… you." He sighed as he rested his forehead against hers. "You're like a drug."

She knew exactly what he meant. She'd thought the same about him. Even as she told herself that she needed to hear him explain himself, she didn't want to miss one moment of his touch.

"I want you, too," she said, running her fingers through his thick curly hair. "It's been..." She took a breath and met his eyes. "A while." She shook her head.

"We should talk," he said, pulling back a little, but she held firm, holding his head close as she tightened her fingers in his hair.

"We will, later," she promised. "But for now, take me to bed."

"Clara—" he started, but she leaned up and covered his words of common sense with her mouth. Her hands tugged his T-shirt free of his jeans, running her fingertips over the tight, toned muscles covered by tanned skin. She'd never been with a man like him before. It was obvious that he spent plenty of time in the gym, and she was going to enjoy every moment she had with him. Even if she grew to regret it later.

When he reached for her tank top, she leaned up and helped him pull it over her head. She hadn't expected to be here with him like this, so she was just wearing a simple white bra. She froze when she remembered she'd skipped pulling on any panties. "Reagan, let's go—" He covered her lips again.

"Here is fine," he started, but she shook her head.

"No, I..." Her eyes moved to the open front door.

He chuckled and sat up quickly. "Okay." He shocked her by hoisting her up into his arms. He moved across the room, nudged the front door shut, and started towards the stairs.

"Aren't you going to lock it?" she asked. He chuckled

instead of answering her, then kissed her again when they hit the landing.

She lost track of where he carried her after that, only surfacing again when her shoulders hit a soft mattress.

"Tell me you have protection," she said between kisses.

"Yes," he agreed. He covered her body with his. "God, you feel so good." He trailed his mouth down her neck as his hands moved over her, lowering to the clasp of her worn shorts. When he tugged them off her hips, he groaned with pleasure. "My god." He leaned back and ran his eyes over her.

"Reagan," she said, reaching for him.

"Hang on, I want to worship you for a moment." He smiled at her. Then with just one fingertip, he trailed a line from her right collarbone to her right hip then slowly crossed over her skin and did the same on the other side. "Perfection," he whispered.

"I need…" She reached for him again, needing to feel his skin against hers, his hands fully on her, powerful, demanding. Instead, he stayed where he was, his eyes running over her slowly with a slight smile playing on his lips.

She leaned up and placed her lips back over his as she reached for the clasp of his jeans. This time, he let her tug him down until his body covered hers, their mouths fused together as their kisses turned desperate.

She tugged his jeans down and dug her nails into his hips, forcing him closer to her body as she wrapped her legs around him. His hands moved over her skin, warming her until he pulled away. She made a small sound in complaint, but his chuckle stopped her, and she opened her eyes.

He tugged off his jeans and pulled a condom from the nightstand before he came back over her.

"This has nothing to do with my job." It was almost a growl as his eyes locked with hers.

"No," she agreed and pulled him back to her.

She arched back as his mouth covered one of her breasts instead of returning to her mouth. Her fingers went to his hair once more as she enjoyed his tongue on her skin. He rolled her nipple and sucked on it until she cried out, wrapping her legs around his.

He moved slightly and slid slowly down her body, trailing his mouth over her ribs, her belly, then burying his face between her legs. She'd never felt anything more wonderful than his mouth on her. Her fists gripped the comforter as she moaned with ecstasy while he pushed a finger into her pussy. She cried out as she lost herself in his touch.

There was nothing more beautiful than slipping into Clara for what he hoped was the first time of many to come. She'd gone lax after a powerful orgasm ripped through her. He'd enjoyed hearing his name on her lips when he'd felt her inner muscles tighten around his fingers.

Now, as he moved further into her, her eyes opened, and she sucked her bottom lip between her teeth. Leaning down, he took the sexy swollen lip into his mouth and sucked on it himself. She tasted like honey and summer, and he didn't think he'd ever want to stop tasting her.

When her fingernails dug into his hips, he started to move, slowly. Her eyes grew huge when he jerked his hips, embedding himself fully into her.

"Reagan…"

He could get used to this, he thought quickly. But then she moved and all thoughts escaped his mind, except the primal need to please.

"Okay?" he asked a while later.

"More than okay." She sighed and snuggled into his chest. "I've gone without that for too long."

He chuckled as his hand roamed lightly over her lower back. "I'm very happy to oblige again anytime."

"I'll take you up on that." She leaned up and looked down into his eyes. "But I have to admit, I'll probably need some food before we try that again."

"I'm with you on that one. I was told there was plenty of food in the fridge. I'll bet one of my mother's lasagnas is in the freezer." He started to get up but took a little time to kiss her softly beforehand. "There, that should hold us over until after we get some food."

He pulled on his jeans and watched her hunt around for her clothes.

"I think they're downstairs," he said with a smirk. "Here." He handed her one of his T-shirts. "That should work for now." She pulled it over her head, and he smiled when it hit mid-thigh on her. "Sexy as hell," he said under his breath.

He found a large pan of frozen lasagna and, after putting it in the oven, found a bag of chips and some guacamole to munch on until the food was hot.

"Want a beer?" he asked her, his head still in the fridge.

"Sure," she answered from behind him. He glanced over his shoulder and watched her pick up her shorts and top from the living room floor, where he'd tossed them earlier. Instead of pulling them on, she sat them on the small table near the bottom of the stairs. She picked up a picture in a frame that sat there.

"Is this you?" she asked, holding the image towards him.

He glanced over and laughed at the image of his father and Uncle Marcus with their arms slung around each other's shoulders, sitting on the porch swing they had built together. The one that still hung out there now. "No, that's my dad. The month he came to live at the Graytons."

"How did he break his arm?" she asked, setting the photo back down.

His mood darkened. "His old man—his real one, I mean—was a boxer and liked to use his kid as a punching bag." He had turned away from her when he'd said this. He opened the bag of chips and tossed some into a large bowl. "His past is the reason my dad started Haven House, a home for wayward children."

"Your parents were raised here? Together?" she asked, causing him to turn around again. She was holding another picture, looking down at it. "This is your mother, right?" She pointed to the image of the entire family together shortly after they had all come to live there.

"Yes." He smiled. "They were both adopted by the Graytons, having come from messed up families."

"Your mother from the cult, your father from an abusive father." She set the picture frame down and walked towards him. "And yet, they all look like they belong together."

"They do." He smiled. "Even my parents." He chuckled and handed her a soda. "There may not be blood between any of them, but they're family. Even my folks. Their relationship goes beyond husband and wife. The way they tell it, from the first moment they met when they were kids, they were in love."

Her eyes met his and he felt his heart kick. For the first time in his life, he knew exactly what his parents had been talking about.

CHAPTER 10

The next morning Clara woke in Reagan's bed, his arms wrapped around her tightly as if he was still in protection mode, even while asleep.

She desperately needed to use the bathroom and tried to figure out how to escape his hold without waking him.

Deciding there wasn't a way, she lifted his arm off her.

"Morning," he said, wrapping both arms around her, causing her to groan.

She wiggled and felt him hard against her stomach. "I have to pee." She escaped his hold.

Shutting the bathroom door on his chuckles, she freshened up, making sure to rinse her mouth out with some of his toothpaste, since her brush was in the other bathroom.

She'd never slept with a man… well, spent a whole night with him. She didn't know what to do or what was expected of her in the morning.

He'd been hard. Did that mean he wanted to… She gasped and lifted her armpit for a sniff inspection. Frowning, she glanced around for something to make her smell better. Not that she stunk. But she desperately wished for her bottle of perfume.

"You okay in there?" he asked from just outside the door.

"Yeah," she called out, trying to figure out how she could explain that she needed her bathroom. Giving up, she opened the door.

He was leaning on the doorjamb, his arm stretched out, blocking her from escaping.

"You look amazing in the morning." He smiled down at her, then before she could dodge him, he leaned in and covered her lips with his. "You taste better than you look," he said against her skin. "Come back to bed." His hands were running up and down her sides as he started walking them towards the bed.

"Reagan, I could use a shower," she said, arching her head back as he trailed kisses down towards her collarbone.

"I want you first, then we can shower." He hoisted her up until her legs wrapped around his hips. Then they were falling back on the bed and she forgot everything except him.

She'd never showered with anyone before and was thankful the shower in his bathroom was bigger than the one in hers. Still, he filled up most of the space with his broad shoulders.

He was gentle as he washed her hair and rinsed it, then continued to run soapy hands over her body, making sure to clean every inch of her.

She disappeared into her room to wash her face before heading down the stairs.

He was standing at the stove flipping a pancake when

she sat at the bar and watched him. Her eyes were glued to his back as he worked and her mind wandered.

She'd always dreamed of having a man like Reagan. Well, fantasized about it, at any rate. Yet she'd never really imagined she'd find someone so caring, so gentle, and yet so strong. Someone she trusted.

Just thinking about trust had her gazing out the windows as she thought about her own family.

What did they think about her? She knew that her leaving and going into hiding probably made them believe she'd killed Gina. Hell, her memories of that night were nothing but a blur, so she could have. But something in her gut told her she hadn't. She'd loved Gina.

Looking back, she couldn't remember one fight between them. But she also couldn't remember going to her sister's graduation earlier that evening. It was as if that entire day had been wiped from her memories.

What she did remember was waking up with something sticky covering her arms as someone stood over her screaming. Her stepmother, Rebecca, had gone into her father's office to get the gift they had purchased for Gina and found them.

Clara had gotten to her knees, ripping her party dress and slipping in the fluid that covered her entire body. When she'd glanced down at her hands, her mind had gone blank, seeing them a deep red.

She'd look down at Gina's dark eyes as they stared up at her without blinking. After that, she'd simply shut down. Since she was still on her knees, she hadn't fallen over. Instead, she'd rested her hands on the edge of her father's desk as people rushed into the room.

She remembered her father's voice as he called to her while her stepmother screamed.

"What did you do?" she yelled over and over at her.

She was shuffled around, pushed into a chair, then a blanket was tossed over her shoulders.

The police came and she was ushered out of the house. After that, she was questioned until her head felt dull and she started slurring her words. Even then, she remained in a bright room and was only given water to drink as the police tried to get her to confess to something she had no memory of.

There were times she thought of just giving in and telling them something, anything, so she could get some rest. The skin they found under her fingernails was tested for DNA, and her clothes were taken from her for evidence.

Almost thirty hours after being brought into the police station, she was hustled back out by her father, his thick black raincoat covering her head as reporters shouted questions at them.

She spent a day at home, locked in her room, afraid to venture downstairs. Then, when her stepmother was at the store and her father was at the office, she'd packed up a bag of her belongings and disappeared.

"You're deep in thought." Reagan broke into her thoughts as he set a plate of pancakes in front of her. He sat next to her with his own plate. "Anything you'd like to share?"

"Just thinking about the past." Her stomach knotted as the memories started to fade.

"About your sister?" he asked, putting his fork down and turning towards her. "Want to talk about it?"

~

At first, Reagan didn't think Clara would say anything. But then she surprised him by turning towards him.

"I told you that she died," she started slowly.

"Yes," he agreed when she didn't continue. He picked up her hands and started rubbing them. They were ice cold and when he looked into her eyes, he could tell she was struggling to find the right words. "Just say it," he said softly. "I can see you're struggling."

Her eyes met his and she took a deep breath. "I… they found me next to her body. The murder weapon, an award my father had gotten the previous year, had my bloodied fingerprints all over it." He waited, already knowing all of the information. Still, seeing her describe the details allowed him to get an insider look that none of the reports or interviews could have. "I… was unconscious when my stepmother came in to my father's office. I… must have passed out. But her blood was everywhere." She looked down at her hands now as if she could still see the blood on them.

"You could have been knocked unconscious," he suggested, even though he'd read the medical examiner's report that she had no visible wounds, a detail that would eventually free her from police custody, since Gina had obviously scratched her assailant.

"No." She shook her head. "I was fine. Nothing was wrong with me." She closed her eyes and he felt her shiver. "I can't remember most of that day, up until I woke next to her."

He frowned. That little detail wasn't in any reports. "Did you tell the police that?" he asked.

Her eyes opened and focused on him. "N-no." She shrugged. "It wouldn't have done any good."

"Did they do a blood test on you?" he asked, knowing already there hadn't been one in her police file. "To see if there was anything in your system. Something that would explain the memory loss?"

"No." She sighed. "They kept me in questioning so long." She rested on the counter.

"Clara." He waited until her attention was on him fully. "There are a lot of things that can interfere with memories."

"I didn't take anything," she said in defense.

"No," he agreed. "But something could have been slipped into your drink. It was a party, right?"

"Yes," she agreed and tilted her head, "but nothing can wipe memories beforehand. Someone would have had to slip me something in my breakfast, since I don't remember anything that day until I woke up on the floor."

"Lots of them can." He moved over to retrieve his laptop. Moving his full plate aside, he started searching for them.

While they ate, he ran through a list of the top ten over-the-counter drugs that could cause memory loss.

"I never knew there were so many pills that could do something like that," she admitted.

"And those are just the over-the-counter ones. If we search prescriptions..." He did and they both groaned. "Yeah," he agreed and shut his laptop down. "But without a blood test right after, nothing can be proven."

"Who would want to slip me pills to make me forget?" she asked, standing up and taking both of their plates to the sink.

"The same person who killed your sister," he answered.

Her hands stilled and he watched the plates teeter in them. Rushing over, he steadied her and set his grandfather's favorite plates on the counter next to the sink.

"Easy," he told her and wrapped her in his arms. "We'll figure this out, together," he promised her and kissed the top of her head.

One thing was clear to Reagan after spending some more time with her—Clara Cruz had had nothing to do with her sister's death. Someone had tried, and failed, to frame her for murder.

Just then, the back door opened, and his uncle Marcus walked in carrying an armful of grocery bags. He was followed by his other uncles, Cole and Luke, all of them weighted down with bags.

"Oops," Marcus said when he noticed them in the embrace. He immediately tried to back out of the door, but bumped solidly into Cole, who lost his hold on one of his bags.

Cans of soups spilled out of the reusable grocery bags his grandfather used.

"Hey, watch it," Cole said, shoving his brother. "You have to tell Dad why you bent his cans."

"What's the hold up?" Luke asked as he tried to step all of the way in. "Oh," he said after seeing Clara jump out of his hold. "Oops."

By this time Cole had spotted them and smiled. "Does our dad know you've got a woman in his house?"

"I'm the one who told the boy to bring her here in the first place," his grandfather said from the front door. "And

I thought I told you boys to be careful." He nodded to the spilled groceries.

"It was Marcus' fault." Cole pointed to his brother.

"Tattletale," Marcus said under his breath as he stabbed Cole with an elbow. "Where do you want these, Dad?" he asked, recovering.

"I…" Clara glanced down at his T-shirt, which she was still wearing, and without another word, sprinted towards the stairs.

"Look what you did now, Cole. You've gone and scared her away," Marcus joked.

"Me?" Cole set his remaining bag down on the countertop. "I don't cause women to run away from me. I make them swoon."

Just then, someone cleared their throat from the doorway.

Wendy Grayton stood with her hands on her hips as she watched her husband.

"Busted," Luke joked and started to pick up the spilled groceries.

"What I meant to say was… I used to make them swoon." Cole rushed over and wrapped his wife in his arms playfully, kissing her until she laughed and slapped at his shoulders.

"Who was that?" Marcus asked, moving to his side.

"Clara," he answered, his eyes going towards the empty staircase.

"We didn't mean to spook her," he added.

"You didn't." He smiled and pushed his uncle on the shoulder, almost toppling the man over. "You're too weak to spook anyone."

It was an old game he and his uncles played. One he'd

lost until he'd hit his last growth spurt and then bulked out in the military. Now he could easily take any of them down, if he wanted to.

Marcus shoved back, and they started to wrestle, until his grandfather stepped into the room.

"Not in the house," he said softly, causing them to still.

"Sorry," Reagan said, rushing to help put away the groceries. Then his dad walked in with a large cooler. "What's all this food for?" he asked, seeing that the cooler was full of fish that his uncles and father had no doubt caught.

"We're having a fish fry," his father answered. "Everyone will be over in a couple hours."

"We've got plenty to do to get ready," his grandfather added. "So." He turned to him. "Why don't you go on up and get dressed." He nodded to his bare chest and jeans. "You and Clara can help."

Looking around the room, he understood what this was. This was his family's way of telling him and Clara that she was accepted into the family.

The Grayton family had just picked up another lost soul to rescue.

CHAPTER 11

*S*he had never met friendlier people in her life. Even when she'd lived at home, her parents had never had a family gathering that made her feel as warm and accepted as the Grayton family did.

She hadn't laughed this hard in years. All of his aunts and uncles had arrived as well as his cousins: Lizzy, Karen, Rose, and the only other male in the group, Kade.

She'd been told the only one missing was Reagan's sister, Bella, as everyone referred to her.

Reagan had mentioned that his sister was away at college in Arizona but was going to be home the following weekend.

Everyone moved around the house preparing for the large meal. When it got too hot, they all walked down to the pond and, to her slight surprise, stripped down to their boxers and underwear and jumped in. Every single one, even Reagan's grandfather.

Since all of his aunts and cousins had done it, she

peeled off her clothes, thankful she'd chosen a black bra and matching panties this time and joined them.

Then they all lay around on the sand and told stories of how they used to catch bullfrogs in the pond.

When the sun started sinking lower, a big silver pot was dragged out to the back porch. Slices of fish were placed in the thick dark sizzling oil. Most of the men stood around it like they were watching the latest game on the set. Clara helped get the rest of the meal together in the kitchen while sipping a glass of wine someone had handed her.

She was asked how she met Reagan and quickly told everyone the story, answering more questions as they worked.

Food was served and eaten on the back patio as the sun cast warm shadows over the yard and pond waters.

They were all sitting around the table when Reagan's phone went off. When he stiffened next to her, she glanced over and happened to catch the name on the screen.

Reagan looked over at her briefly before getting up and walking into the house to take the call from her father.

All conversation seemed to stop while her eyes remained glued to the back door. It wasn't until he walked back out that she realized just how nervous she'd been, knowing he might be in there telling her father where she was.

Did this mean she had to return home? What if her father caught a plane out here? Could she handle it if Reagan's family knew about what she'd been accused of?

Standing up quickly, she wrapped her arms around herself and walked away from the group, knowing that Reagan would follow her and fill her in.

They ended up back at the pond's edge.

"This is a magical place," she said under her breath. "Here, I've allowed myself to forget everything." She closed her eyes as Reagan wrapped his arms around her. "I feel as if I could just let go of… well, everything. Like I could actually be happy again."

"You can," he said softly. He placed a kiss on her forehead. "Soon," he promised. "You know we have to go. We can't let whoever did this get away."

She leaned back and looked up at him. Her eyes scanned his face. What she saw there was determination. It made her realize that for the past five years, she'd been so selfish. Not once had she thought about who had killed her sister and gotten away with it. Instead, she'd only been focused on her own suffering, her loss of Gina.

Straightening her shoulders, she nodded. "How do you intend on catching a murderer?" she asked.

"Well, to catch a fish, you use bait," he answered as he ran his hands over her arms. "I'm going to hate it, but I'm going to deliver you home, then appear to disappear from your life."

She frowned. "This isn't just your way of getting me off your hands is it?" she asked, earning a chuckle from him.

"If I wanted you out of my life, I never would have introduced you to my family." He smiled. "You're stuck like a fly in molasses now."

She smiled. "I'm assuming your family is the molasses?"

"Yeah." He bent down and kissed her. "Sorry, I should have warned you. The Graytons suck in lost souls and spit out happy families."

She liked the sound of that, being part of his family. Glancing back towards the lighted house, where laughter could be heard echoing over the field, she could just imagine returning. Actually, she could imagine staying here forever, but since she didn't want to freak Reagan out, she kept that to herself and leaned up and kissed him instead.

The following morning, they climbed into his truck and made their way towards the airport. He'd booked their flights last night as she slept beside him, sated from a happy day, great conversation, a good meal, and easily the best sex she'd had in her life.

She was nervous on the flight across the States. They had a long layover in Atlanta and spent almost three hours walking around the massive airport. When they finally jumped onto their plane to Denver, she was exhausted and slept until they landed. They had to run to their connecting flight and made it just in time.

On the last flight, she was too nervous to sleep and kept glancing at her watch as they moved across time zones, getting them closer and closer to her home. No, she corrected her thoughts, what used to be her home. She could no longer imagine a life in California.

When she thought about her future, she only envisioned being with Reagan. Anywhere. She didn't want to face her past or her family without him by her side. Even though they had only known each other a few days, she felt deep down that it was just… right.

Reagan watched Clara stand stiff as her stepmother rushed

towards her and hugged her. They had walked in silence up the front steps of the mega mansion her father lived in. When Rebecca Cruz had opened the door instead of Clara's father, he'd been curious to see how the woman would react.

He'd seen plenty of actors in his past, but something about the woman made it hard for him to read her. The squeal she'd let out had been for show, but the emotions she'd put into holding onto Clara had been real.

"Rebecca, what is…" Clara's father stepped into the doorway. Reagan watched the man's face go pale, then he too was holding onto Clara.

"Mr. and Mrs. Cruz." He broke the silence after a moment.

They released Clara and motioned for them to go inside. He noticed that her father glanced around outside as if to see if anyone had noticed the exchange.

He'd been in the house before, when he'd been hired. Since Gina's death, Clara's father had been working strictly from his home office. He'd heard rumors that the man had hardly left the space where his youngest daughter had last been alive. He'd even taken a step back from running his business, leaving his business partner, Henry Knight, to run things instead.

Even though Carlo Cruz had created the massive real estate company, just two years after hitting it big he'd hired the man, which had taken the business to a different level.

As the four of them settled in the living room, he continued to watch Clara's parents to see how they were dealing with her being back.

Clara, for her part, looked stiff and uncomfortable. He

noticed a few times that her eyes darted towards a pair of doors down a long hallway and figured that was her father's office.

The house was all glass and angles, with windows that looked out over the city lights. There was a massive swimming pool that sat directly outside of a wall of glass doors that were currently open, allowing the evening breeze to cool off the room.

The home was a complete contrast to the one he'd grown up in.

"Please, sit." Her father motioned to one of the matching white leather sofas facing each other. He sat down and immediately Clara sat beside him.

He desperately wished to reach over and touch her, but they had agreed to their plan and instead he laced his fingers together and rested his elbows on his knees, while her parents took a seat on the opposite sofa.

"Where have you been all this time?" her father asked, concern lacing his voice.

Clara cleared her voice, then glanced at him quickly before answering. "Florida," she said simply.

He knew she'd spent the last five years jumping around the States but had indeed spent the last year of it in Florida.

"Why?" her stepmother asked. "Why did you leave us?"

"I… needed time to myself. I had to…" Clara shook her head. "I couldn't…" She glanced towards those doors again. "I can't…" She jumped up and rushed from the room, heading out the glass wall towards the backyard.

Her father instantly jumped up, but Rebecca stopped

him. "No, let me go," she said softly and then disappeared out the doors.

Being left alone with her father, he decided to get their plan into motion.

"Mr. Cruz, you've paid me to find your daughter." He motioned towards the backyard. "But your daughter has hired me to find out all I can about that night."

He watched her father's reaction. He'd expected surprise. What he hadn't expected was annoyance. He had been sure the man would want to know everything he could about the death of his daughter.

"The police have already gone over everything. There's nothing else. It's in the past." He closed his eyes and took a few deep breaths. "Gina is gone. No amount of looking into that night is going to bring my daughter back." His eyes went to the backyard and changed, filling with love instead. "I need to protect my daughter," he said softly. "Of course, I'll pay you for your time, but this ends here." He stood up and Reagan followed him back into his office to receive his final payment.

It was hard taking the man's check, especially since what he wanted to do was run outside, gather Clara in his arms, and take her away from this huge mess.

Instead, he tucked the check into his pocket, then allowed himself to be ushered out of the home without even saying goodbye to Clara.

CHAPTER 12

Clara lay in her own bed for the first time in five years and cried herself to sleep.

Reagan had texted her but so far, she hadn't replied. Instead, she stared at her screen and thought of how to answer him.

How was she doing? She was alive while Gina wasn't. It was hard. In the past five years, she'd thought so much of her sister, but being home… She glanced around and ghosts of her sister and the past flooded her mind. She typed:

-I miss you.

Before she could double back, she hit send.

-God, I miss you so much. I wish I could hold you.

-What did my dad say?

When she'd returned inside with Rebecca, Reagan had been gone. Her father had told her that he'd been paid and that his job was over.

She'd told him that she'd hired Reagan to find out about that night.

"I know, he told me." Her dad had crossed the room and taken her shoulders. It was a move she knew all too well. One that said, I'm in charge and I'll take care of everything. She wanted to push him away and yell. Instead, she followed Reagan's plan and allowed her father to shuffle her upstairs and into her bedroom for the night.

-He told me that he didn't want anyone digging up the past.

-What do you think that means?

She frowned while she waited for his reply.

-I think it means that he wants to protect you.

She let that sink in. Why would he need to protect her? The only reason she could think of was that he thought she had something to do with Gina's death. Her father believed that she had killed her sister. More tears rolled down her face.

-Clara, he loves you. I'm sure he doesn't believe… hell, I wish I was there, holding you.

She set her phone down and tucked herself into a ball. She heard it chime with new messages but just couldn't muster up the strength or the will to open her eyes again.

She woke when someone entered her room. Thinking it was her father, she rolled away.

Instead, strong arms gathered her up and held her while she started crying again. She must be dreaming, she thought. Reagan wasn't really here.

"I'm here," he said softly into her ear.

"Reagan?" She jerked back and looked through the darkness into his eyes. He chuckled. "Yeah. For a high-dollar mansion, this place is pretty easy to break into." He brushed a strand of her hair away from her face.

She smiled and wrapped her arms around him, already

feeling more stable than before. "You're here," she said again, mainly just to reassure herself.

"I am." He kissed the top of her head and held her tighter. "I don't know how I'm going to get out, but for now, I'm here."

She needed him, needed him to take all of her pain away. Reaching up, she placed her lips over his and relished in the desire that flooded her, feeling his instant flash of hunger, which matched her own.

They tugged at clothes, pulling and pushing until they were both naked. She wanted, no, needed the speed. Pushing on his chest, she forced him to lie back as she climbed onto his hips and slid over him. His groan was low and primitive sounding as she started to move over him. His fingers dug into her hips, guiding her, holding her as she took what she needed. When they moved up to cup her breasts, she leaned in and kissed him until she felt herself slipping.

He rolled slightly, keeping their bodies connected as he took over, pumping fast and hard into her until she forgot everything except him. Only then did she allow herself to completely lose control.

"I love you." The words slipped out as she sank into darkness.

When she woke, Reagan was gone. Seeing her sheets and comforter in disarray confirmed that he had been there. It hadn't been a dream.

Smiling, she picked up her phone and read his message to her.

-I love you too. You fell asleep before I could say it. I love you. I'll try to see you today. Be safe. Love you.

She smiled as she read the message over and over again.

Then there was a knock on her door, and everything came crashing back down as memories of where she was and why she was there surfaced. How was she going to make it through the day without Reagan?

Reagan spent the day down at Sunset Dreams Realty, melting into the background. At first, he had posed as a prospective buyer, but after seeing how lax the security was in the building, he just hung around the lobby and wandered around the building.

He was slightly surprised when he found out that Henry Knight was out of the office for the week. When he asked for more information, he was told the man had taken some personal time. He made a mental note to look further into the man when he had his laptop.

Around eleven in the morning, he was slightly surprised to see Rebecca Cruz waltz through the lobby of the building and head towards the bank of elevators.

He wanted to follow her, but she knew who he was, and he didn't want her to see him. Instead, he watched as her elevator continued up to the top floor where the executive offices were.

He stayed in the lobby and waited for her to come back down. It was almost an hour later and by the looks of it, the woman had been riled up. She was looking very agitated.

Deciding there wasn't anything more he could learn in the building, he followed her. From there, she drove her white BMW convertible down to Rodeo Drive, where she spent half an hour in Tiffany's and reappeared with several of their iconic blue bags and a smile on her lips.

From there, she met a girlfriend for lunch. He snapped a few pictures of her and her friend sitting under the umbrellas, sipping their champagne while he snacked on a granola bar he'd found at the bottom of his bag and sipped warm water from a water bottle. He didn't mind skipping lunch while he was on the job. He'd had plenty of days where he'd gone without anything during his military days.

This time, his mind kept wandering to what Clara was doing. Was she at home still with her father?

Pulling out his phone, he looked down at the last message he'd left her. Since she hadn't responded, he guessed that she was too busy to respond.

She'd said that she loved him, and he'd told her it in return. He'd never said those words to a woman before, other than family. He didn't know what came next in the relationship, other than seeing each other more often.

He was following her stepmother out of the restaurant when he heard his phone chime. Waiting until they were stopped at a light, he pulled out his phone.

The message was from a blocked number.

-Leave California

-Who is this? he replied, only to get an instant reply.

-Leave now. This is your last chance.

-I'm not going anywhere, not until I find out who you are and who killed Gina Cruz.

He hit send on the message as the stop light turned green and Rebecca's BMW took off. He was two cars behind her and tucked his phone back into his pocket as he started to pull through the intersection.

He spotted the truck from the corner of his eye but instantly knew it was too late to avoid the collision. Jerking the wheel of his rental, he pointed his side of the car away from the oncoming truck as metal hit metal. He watched the front left hood take most of the impact instead of his car door. The hood buckled and twisted, giving way to the heavier vehicle.

His vision was blocked when the windshield shattered into a spiderweb of shards before finally bursting inward towards him.

His chest and face hit the airbags as his seatbelt jerked on his shoulder, burning his skin through the T-shirt he was wearing.

He felt his knee hit the dash, then felt his left ankle wedge as the compartment started to close in on him.

He thought of Clara as his car was pushed through the intersection. It finally rested on the curb, pressed against the pole from the stop lights.

He grunted as he tried unsuccessfully to open his door, then yanked off his seatbelt, leaned over, and tried the passenger side. It was twisted and wedged against the pole, locking him in the vehicle.

He glanced around and saw the truck that had hit him back up. For a split second, he thought the thing was going to ram him again, but instead, it sat there, the engine revved, watching him. The windows were tinted so dark that he could only make out a dark form behind the wheel.

Suddenly, it took off, barreling down the road. He would have gotten the license plate, but the spot where one should be was empty. Cursing, he tried his door again, then froze when he noticed the smoke coming from where the hood was twisted and bent over the engine.

Before he could react, flames burst out and the heat of the fire instantly hit him.

He used his shoulder to pound on the door as he heard people screaming for him to get out. Like he didn't know he was screwed. Both of the car doors were stuck shut due to the impact. His windshield was shattered, and the fire was growing bigger.

Fears of it hitting the gas tank played in his head and, once more, he thought of Clara.

CHAPTER 13

It had been one of the worst days of her life since the day of her sister's murder. Shortly after breakfast was served up by a new maid, one that treated her as if she was a child, her stepmother and father disappeared into his office. She heard raised voices and groaned as memories of their many fights surfaced.

Rebecca had played her mother for longer than her real mother had. She'd liked the woman back when she'd been hired to be her and Gina's nanny.

She'd been there for them after their mother had died. A few years later, both of the sisters had been excited when she'd married their father.

However, shortly after Clara graduated high school and started attending college classes, something had changed. Not just in Rebecca, but in her father as well.

Her dad stopped going into the office every day and chose to spend his days in his home office, alone. This had changed Rebecca as well, since she had been used to having the house to herself and being able to do what she wanted, coming and going. Now it was as if her father made her stepmother account for not only all of her time, but her money as well.

Clara hadn't wanted to know what was up with them at the time. Instead, she'd immersed herself in school. Then Gina's graduation had come.

After Rebecca stormed out of the house shortly after the argument, her father stepped out of the one room in the house that Clara was determined never to go back into.

"What do you say to spending the day with your old man?" Her father had smiled and tried to act cheerful, but Clara could see the frustration and hurt behind his eyes.

"I…" She tried to think of an excuse to spend the day alone, but she knew Reagan's plan and, if it was going to succeed, she needed to spend as much time with her parents as possible. "Sure," she finished, wishing suddenly she was on a small private beach at a little pond with two wet dogs running around splashing her.

Since her father had no clue what she was into, he dragged her down to the mall to shop. For the past five years, she'd avoided malls or even clothes shopping. Instead, she'd hoarded what little money she had left over every paycheck. Now, as her father dragged her from one store to the next, trying to spend more money on her than she'd seen in a year, she felt a bigger disconnection from him than ever.

Had she really enjoyed this at one point? There had been plenty of shopping trips with Gina and their step-mother, and Clara could honestly say she'd never thought about how much money had exchanged hands.

Hell, her closet and bedroom were still packed with items easily worth what she paid in a year for rent.

They sat in a bistro and were served lunch. While she ate her Cobb salad, she realized she missed Rico's greasy fries and grilled gulf shrimp.

After, they drove down to her father's favorite spot along the beach. The drive was nice, but the silence between them stretched on and made the entire ordeal uncomfortable.

She'd asked him about what he'd been doing for the past five years, but when he'd answered with just one-word answers, she'd given up trying.

When they pulled into their long twisting driveway, she had plans to disappear back into her room. But when they entered the house, she was shocked to see a crowd of people in the living room, drinks in their hands as they shouted, "Welcome home!" at her. Instantly, she tensed as she glanced around the room. Here were the people she'd at one time called friends.

Almost every single person smiling at her now had turned their back on her after Gina's murder. Several had even done television interviews claiming that there had always been something off between the sisters.

She turned to her father as her stepmother rushed over to hug her. Her father smiled over at her as if he expected the surprise to be the greatest gift. Instead, she turned on her heels and, without another word, disappeared up the stairs and locked herself in her room.

She'd heard the gasps and gossip starting before she'd climbed all of the stairs, but she no longer cared.

Flinging herself down on her bed, she pulled out her phone and noticed the text from Reagan.

-I hope your day is going better than mine. I miss you. I'll try coming to you again tonight. Love you.

Typing a text back to him through tear-filled eyes, she replied.

-Day sucked. I miss you too. Please come. I need you. Love you.

She waited for his reply. When someone knocked on her door, she ignored it and turned over, laying the phone next to her face so she could see when Reagan texted her back. She woke a few hours later, still tired and confused.

Outside her window it was dark. Her stomach growled loudly, and she realized she'd only had a muffin and half of her Cobb salad to eat all day.

Looking at her phone, she frowned when she noticed Reagan hadn't replied to her last message.

Pulling off her shoes, she changed into a pair of yoga pants and a T-shirt, then tiptoed down the stairs. She was thankful when the house was dark and quiet.

Pulling out a loaf of bread, she quickly made herself a turkey sandwich, then took an entire bag of Ruffles upstairs with her, along with a root beer from the fridge.

She didn't know who it belonged to since her parents didn't drink soda, but she figured since it was there, she'd enjoy it. She wanted something sweet, but the soda would have to do.

Locking her door behind her, she almost screamed with she saw a dark shadow emerge from her window curtain.

"Sorry," Reagan said in a low voice.

She chuckled and quickly set down her meal and rushed to his side.

When she got closer, she gasped and held in a cry at the sight of blood dripping from his forehead. She noticed a thick smell of smoke on his clothes as she rushed closer to him. Besides the cut above his left eye, he was sporting a black eye and his lip was swollen.

He looked like he'd gotten in a fight. Then she watched him limp towards her.

"I'm okay," he said reassuringly as he gathered her up in his arms.

Reagan could have just fallen into Clara's arms and died a happy man. Every part of him hurt. He'd allowed himself to be driven to the local hospital and checked out, where he'd received small bandages for his cuts and some over-the-counter pain pills, which he'd tucked into his pocket and forgotten the moment he stepped out of the hospital.

He'd rented another car, making sure to get the extra insurance again on this one. Then he'd driven up into the hills and climbed the outside stone wall that surrounded her family's home. From there, it was as easy as walking up a set of outside stairs and crawling over an outside balcony to get to Clara's window, which she'd left open again tonight.

But when he'd arrived, her bed had been empty. He'd stood there, in the dark, looking at it as if he expected her to reemerge. When the door had opened, he'd relaxed seeing her step in with food. His stomach instantly reminded him that all he'd eaten that day was the granola bar.

Now, he held onto her, his stomach and his desire for food forgotten completely.

When her arms tightened slightly around him, pain shot up his bruised ribs, causing him to groan with pain.

"I'm sorry." She jumped back from him and rushed over to turn on the lamp by her bed. When she saw him in the light, she gasped even louder. "What happened?" she cried, rushing back over to him and touching his forehead and lip softly.

"Car accident," he answered as she tugged him towards the bed. He figured it was best to keep the details from her.

"Oh my," she said under her breath. "Are you hurt?" She ran her eyes over him. "Anything broken?"

"No, just bruised."

She reached up and touched the small bandage over his cut. "Stitches?"

"No." He sighed as his hands reached for her again.

"Let me clean you up." She motioned to the dried blood covering his face.

"I'd kill for a shower and some clean clothes." He nodded to the bag they had pried from the back of the burned-out car.

"Okay." She tugged on his hands and he followed her into her bathroom. It had been too dark last night to see her room and, to be honest, he'd only been thinking about being with her and hadn't noticed anything else. Now, however, he appreciated the simplicity of her taste.

Soft white sheets and comforter covered her bed, and a cream-colored chair sat in the corner of her room. There were a few college posters on her walls, but for the most part, the place was classy.

Her bathroom was bigger than anything he'd seen before. The shower alone was the size of his whole bathroom. It had a long wooden bench, like a sauna. The glass walls enclosing it reached all the way from the floor to the twelve-foot ceiling. There was a jet tub sitting in front of a massive window opposite a wall of cabinets and counter-tops, which held two sinks.

She nudged him to sit on the countertop while she searched the drawers for a cloth, then opened a large mirror and pulled out a bottle of hydrogen peroxide.

"I'm fine," he explained, not wanting to feel the sting on any of the many burns and cuts he had covering his arms and face.

He'd made the mistake of holding out his hands, allowing her to see the burns on them.

She gasped again and almost dropped the bottle. "Did you catch on fire?" she said, frowning down at him.

"Almost." He groaned when he remembered how close it had been. He'd left the hospital with bandages on his hands but tossed them since they kept getting in his way.

She took his hands in hers and frowned down at them. "You need to keep something on these," she said as a tear fell from her eyes and landed on his sizzled skin.

He gathered her once more in his arms and just held on as she cried for his scorched and bruised skin. He'd never cared so much about someone as he did about Clara.

"Baby, don't cry," he begged as he held her.

"You're… someone did this to you." She pulled back. "I can see it in your eyes. You're keeping it from me." She shook her head. "Don't. I'm strong enough to know."

He smiled and wiped the tears gently from her eyes. "You are." He kissed her softly, since his lip was split and any more pressure would open it again. "I love you. When this is over, I'm going to take you somewhere. Just the two of us. Alone."

She nodded her head. "Yes, please." She sighed and

held onto him. "First, you need a shower." She pulled away again, her nose crinkled up at the stench emanating from his clothes.

He couldn't stop the chuckle, or the desire to pull her into the massive shower with him.

By the time they crawled into her bed, he had revised their plans to expose her sister's killer.

CHAPTER 14

Clara woke to a gasp and for one split second, she thought she was back on the floor of her father's office. Her entire body jerked, then she felt the heavy arm resting over her chest, holding her down to the soft mattress.

Looking around, she glanced at the door where her stepmother stood, a tray of food in her hands as she gaped at them lying naked on her bed.

Her stepmother's eyes ran over Reagan and for a split second, she saw desire and appreciation in her eyes.

Reaching down, she pulled the sheets over both of them and yelled, "Get out."

Rebecca's eyes narrowed on her as she walked over and set the tray of food down on her desk. "You didn't have dinner." She turned and noticed the empty plate and bag of chips Reagan had finished off last night. "Guess you helped yourself after all." She turned on her heels and strode out of the room, making sure to shut it softly behind her, but not before she called over her shoulder. "I'm sure

Carlo will want to talk to you when you're dressed. Both of you."

"We did it now." Clara groaned and covered her face with the sheets.

"No." Reagan tugged the sheets down. The fact that he was smiling at her had her frowning even more. "I did. While you slept, I… revised the plan." He shrugged.

"This?" She waved to the door and sat up. "This was your new plan?"

"Well, I had hoped to remember to pull the sheets over us, but yeah." He smiled and leaned in to kiss her. "It is." He jumped up from the bed, still fully naked as he walked over to the tray of food. After sniffing the orange juice, he downed half of the glass.

Since her eyes were locked on his toned ass, she didn't argue when he stood there and ate her breakfast.

He filled her in on his new plan while they dressed. When they walked down the stairs, hand in hand, she was more nervous about this plan than the first one. Before, she was the only one exposed. Now Reagan was going to take the heat. But after yesterday, she knew that he was already in too deep to avoid getting burned. She took his charred hands and raised her chin as they stepped into the kitchen where her father was sitting, waiting for them. It was obvious by the look on his face that Rebecca had already filled him in about who she was with.

"I paid you to find my daughter, not to sleep with her." Her father almost yelled it. His face was red, like it always got when he was angry.

"You did," Reagan said calmly. "This"—he held up their joined hands— "has nothing to do with the job."

"The hell it doesn't. I'll be damned if I'm going to

stand by and let you sneak into this household when we're broken. Clara's in a fragile state right now. The last thing she needs is someone sniffing around because of what's in her pocketbook." To her horror, her father pulled out his checkbook. "How much are you wanting?" he asked as he started writing.

For a split second, she feared of a future without Reagan in it.

"There isn't enough money in the world to make me step away now," Reagan said softly as he squeezed her hand.

Her father threw the pen down on the table. "Out," he growled.

"Fine," she said and turned to go with Reagan.

"Not you," her father shouted. "We just got you back. You are not leaving here."

"Then neither is Reagan," she said calmly.

"Carlo, what does it matter," her stepmother stepped in, laying a hand on her father's shoulder as she smiled across the room at them. "If it's real then it will last. If not…" She shrugged as her eyes ran over Reagan, as if she was remembering what he looked like naked in her bed. "Besides, you've already removed her from your will, so it's not like he'll inherit anything. And her shares of the business are jointly owned by you, and you've locked them up so she can't get her hands on them."

Clara froze, her eyes going to her father. This was news to her. Not that she wanted a dime of his, but to be disowned… It only confirmed her belief that her father believed she was guilty of killing Gina.

She would have thought that the news would have more tears flowing from her eyes. Instead, she vibrated with anger. Dropping Reagan's hand, she moved closer to her father.

"You've disowned me?" she asked in an eerily calm tone.

"He has. Shortly before you returned home. We didn't know what sort of trouble you'd get yourself into and couldn't afford to be dragged down with you," Rebecca answered. Clara turned to her, her eyes burning into the other woman's.

"So, you both think I'm guilty, is that it?" She glared across the glass table at the pair of them. "What I find strange is, instead of standing behind the innocent, you avoid finding Gina's real killer. It's like you don't care who it is, as long as you protect your precious name and business."

She turned back to Reagan, who was smiling at her with pride in his eyes. He held out his hand for hers, and she took it before glancing back at her parents.

"Don't worry, we don't want a thing from you. We'll find Gina's murderer without your help. Then you can sleep comfortably at night knowing the real killer is locked up and that you've lost your only daughter in the process."

She tugged on Reagan's hand and they walked out the front door together.

"I guess it's a good thing I brought out our bags before we headed down the stairs," he said, picking up both of their bags from the balcony outside her bedroom before they headed down to his parked car, just outside of the gates.

"Yeah," she said softly. He'd been trying to lighten the mood, but he knew there was little he could do now.

Her family had chosen. The fact that they hadn't chosen her would sting for the rest of her life.

The only thing he could do now was to be there for her.

They drove out of the Hollywood Hills towards the hotel he'd gotten but had yet to spend a night at.

"What happens now?" she asked as he drove.

He sighed. "Now comes the hard work. I've already reached out to our lawyer."

"We're really going to sue my father for my shares of the business?" she asked.

"Yes." He took her hand as he drove. "If this is about money, if someone killed your sister because of it, then we no longer have a target on us because your father has disowned you. That's assuming that whoever did this learns quickly what happened. If they do, they would have to be in his inner circle. Regardless, we need there to be a target on you."

"It's the principle of the thing," she added, feeling her anger boil even more. "He gave me those shares when I turned eighteen. I'm sure Gina was about to receive hers as well the night…" She closed her eyes and he squeezed her hand.

"Don't think about it," he said softly.

"If she was murdered because of them"—she opened her eyes— "does that mean my father was in on it?"

"No." He frowned. "I really do believe your father thinks you were behind Gina's death."

Her shoulders sank. He hadn't meant to hurt her, but

she needed to believe her father wasn't a murderer, just an elitist and an untrusting bastard.

"How do we find out who killed her? I can't remember anything about that night."

"By flushing the murderer out. You said that all of your friends were there last night?" he asked.

"Yes." She groaned, and he could tell she was replaying the horrible night over again.

"Would you say that it was the same group that was at Gina's graduation party?"

Clara bit her bottom lip as she thought about it. "A few of Gina's close friends were missing, but yes. For the most part, we had the same group of friends."

"Okay, so they all know you're back in town. What we need to do is get you in the spotlight. Think you can stomach a few lunch dates?" he asked her.

This time when she groaned, he knew it was at the annoyance of having to put up with shallow backstabbers.

While he drove, she texted what used to be her closest friend, who happened to be the biggest gossiper of the group.

"Okay." She set her phone down as they pulled into the hotel parking lot. "Brunch tomorrow morning is all set." She leaned back in the seat. "You're staying at the Four Seasons?" she asked with a frown.

He glanced up at the tall building. "I am. It wouldn't be to our plan's benefit if you were staying at a Best Western. Even though I normally do when I'm working," he added with a smile, straining his cracked lip.

He pulled on his sunglasses and carried their bags up to their room.

"We have a full day before I'm supposed to meet

Holly," she said, running her eyes over him. "What do you say to helping me release some of this stress by spending the day in bed with me?" Leaning up, she placed her lips over his, and he felt as if he could do anything as long as she continued to look at him the way she was now.

CHAPTER 15

There was little Clara could do to keep from yelling at her old best friend, Holly, except for biting her bottom lip. She pasted on a fake smile as the girl walked across the parking lot in silver high-heel Jimmy Choo's, a slim black-and-white pencil skirt, and a crisp white blouse.

Clara knew that the entire outfit, including the Gucci bag, had been paid for by Holly's father, Emilio Rhi. The man was a director of some of the best movies to come out of Hollywood over the past two decades.

Growing up, Clara and Holly had almost been one word on everyone's lips. The girls had always been together. So, naturally, it had stung after Gina's murder when Holly hadn't returned any of her texts or calls. It was as if her best friend had wanted to avoid any contact with her.

She was actually shocked that Holly had been at her parents' house the other night and had answered her texts.

Holly air-kissed her as if they had last seen one another a few days ago, instead of years ago.

"I was so worried," she said, running her eyes over the new outfit Clara's father had purchased for her just yesterday. "You look fabulous." She wrapped her arm through hers and started walking towards the front doors of the country club's restaurant. They had spent more time at the place while going through college then they had their own homes.

"Thanks," Clara said, trying to jump back into how the old her would feel having a brunch date with her best friend. "Are those new?" she asked and nodded to the set of rings on her right hand.

"Daniel bought them for me," she gushed, glancing down at the rings. "I was shocked," she said after they had been seated. "Afraid that he was giving me an engagement ring. Thankfully, not." She showed Clara the three matching rings with pink diamonds. "After all, Daniel and I only met a few months ago." She giggled. "I'd never marry a man who I didn't know for more than a year." She placed her drink order and dismissed the waitress after Clara ordered the same. "What about you?" Holly asked and finally gave her all of her attention. "Have you met someone special? Is that why you stayed away for so long?"

Clara thought about how she'd spent the last five years. About why she'd spent them alone. Instead of opening up to what was supposed to be her best friend, she lied.

"Yes, I've met the most wonderful man." She added a sigh of appreciation into the act. "Reagan Grayton's family is from Florida. They're in real estate as well."

"Oh, how wonderful. I bet your dad and stepmom are happy you're back."

"We're only visiting. Reagan and I are staying at the Four Seasons." She dropped the hotel name like Reagan had mentioned she should. "We'll be here for a few more weeks. Until I can cash out my stocks in my father's company."

Holly's eyebrows shot up. "You're selling those off? Why on earth would you?"

"Memories." She glanced around allowing some of the truth to slip into her act. "Too many of them around here."

Holly was silent. Then she surprised her by reaching across the table and taking Clara's hand in hers. "I'm really sorry. I loved Gina like she was my little sister. I know you had nothing to do with her death." Holly closed her eyes, but for a moment beforehand, Clara could see the hurt and emotions. "My dad… He wouldn't let me contact you… after… Then by the time I found out you'd left…" She looked into her eyes again, and Clara could see the truth. It had killed Holly as much as Clara. "I tried to find you. God." Holly reached up and swiped at a tear that had rolled down her face. "I really have missed you." She squeezed her hand and for the first time in five years, Clara realized that she hadn't lost everything from her past.

For the rest of the brunch, Clara's act slipped a little. Still, she was able to get out the vital information she had agreed to drop. After all, Holly may have changed a little in the past five years, but under it all, she was still the same girl who loved to gossip. Most of their lunch was spent with her filling Clara in on what everyone had been up to.

When she left Holly in the parking lot, she met Reagan in the same spot he'd parked beforehand.

"How did it go?" he asked, leaning over and placing a soft kiss on her lips.

His black eye was even darker now, but his lip was almost back to its normal size. The cut on his forehead had started to bruise around it. Somehow all of the bruises and cuts made him look even sexier than before.

"It went." She rested back in the seat.

"You have a few minutes before Emily gets here for drinks," he added, looking at his watch.

She groaned. "Why did we set these all up for today?"

He took her face in his hands. "Because we need to flush out the killer quickly. I'm tired of waiting. I don't think I can handle another attack like the one yesterday. Besides, you've waited over five years."

She straightened and nodded. He was right. She could do this. She only had two more friends to see today. The first was Emily Stark, whose father, Roger, worked with Holly's dad. She and Clara and Holly had hung out together, along with a fourth friend, Terry Knight. Emily had always been more friendly with Holly, but still, they had all hung out together, with Gina as a tagalong. She was meeting Terry for pre-dinner drinks.

Terry's father had been working with Clara's father for as long as Clara could remember. She'd become friends with her because every time their families got together, Terry was always brought along. It wasn't as if Clara hadn't liked her, but it was more of a friendship out of family obligation rather than what she had with Holly and Emily. Still, everywhere they went, Terry had been there.

Drinks with Emily were even more strained than her

lunch with Holly, mainly because Clara knew that Emily had done a few interviews after she'd taken off. Her once friend had gone on camera and claimed that she'd seen Clara and Gina fighting one time over a boy. A boy who she couldn't even name. The lie had not only been huge, but most of Clara's other close friends had squashed the rumor and made Emily look very bad in the public's eyes.

Emily acted much like Holly had at first—as if nothing had happened between them and only a few days had passed since they had last seen one another.

Clara dropped the same hints to Emily as she had with Holly, telling her that was selling her stocks and staying at the Four Seasons.

By the time she met Terry for pre-dinner drinks, she was exhausted. They'd gone back to the hotel so Clara could change into a little blue dress she hadn't seen in five years.

When she entered the club, she scanned the room for Terry and was slightly surprised when she noticed Holly and Emily sitting in a private booth with Terry.

She thought about turning around and running, but then Holly spotted her and waved her across the room.

"This is a surprise," she said, pasting on the same fake smile she'd worn all day.

"Terry texted us and told us you two were meeting for drinks and we thought we'd join in the fun," Holly answered easily.

"Like old times," Emily added, raising her glass and then sipping.

The waitress walked over and took Clara's order. She wanted water but knew that she couldn't get away with something healthy. Not around this group. So instead she sipped a vodka club soda and pretended to have the time of her life with what were now complete strangers.

Reagan watched Clara from across the room. Seeing her interact with her three friends, he could just imagine how she'd been before. The last five years had changed her. So much so that he could tell that she was having a hard time relaxing around the three women who used to make up her world.

He thought about getting closer to her so maybe he could overhear some of their conversation, but then he noticed the guy watching the group. All of his attention turned to the man as he stalked the women.

When the four of them moved to the dance floor, the man followed. Once they were back in the booth, settled with new drinks, he pulled out his phone and snapped a picture and shot it over to Clara.

-Do you know this guy?

He watched as she pulled out her phone and leaned away to look at the picture, making sure that it was angled so that no one else could see her screen.

He watched her face and noticed the moment she saw the photo. He knew instantly that she did know the man. She scanned the crowd until she found the man watching her before answering his text.

-His name is Corey Wells. He's my ex-boyfriend.

Since Clara had locked eyes with him, the guy had taken it as a hint to walk over to the group.

Reagan watched their interaction from across the room. When the man leaned in and placed a kiss on Clara's cheek, he was up from the barstool and halfway across the room before he could think his actions through.

He trusted Clara, but the guy had been stalking her all night.

"Hey," Reagan said as he approached and sat next to Clara before Corey could take the spot. "I got out of the meeting sooner than I thought." He smiled at her and wrapped his arm around her shoulders. "Are these your friends you were telling me about?"

He'd felt Clara tense, but when his arm went around her, she relaxed.

"Yes, Reagan, this is Holly, Emily, Terry, and Corey." She motioned to each. "This is Reagan Grayton."

"Oh." Holly clapped her many-ringed fingers. "This is your guy." She held out her hands for him to take. "What happened to you?" She motioned to his face.

"Car accident," he said with a shrug. "I hate California drivers." He chuckled.

"I hope you weren't hurt too bad," Terry added in.

"Any accident I walk away from is a good one." He watched Corey sit across from Clara. He could tell the guy wanted to talk to her alone, but as long as he was there, it wasn't going to happen.

"Clara was just filling us in on the past five years," Holly started after she waved for another round and the waitress took his and Corey's orders. "But she left out how long you two have known each other."

"What's it been now?" He turned to Clara, letting her fill them in and tell them whatever she wanted. It didn't matter to him. As far as he was concerned, every moment of his life had been a prequel to meeting her, building up to the moment he'd seen her at Rico's place.

"Just over a year," she said easily and took his free hand. "We met where I'm living in Florida."

"Oh? Miami?" Corey jumped in.

"No," Clara started to answer but he jumped in.

"The Panhandle," he answered, wanting to keep it vague. "What do you do, Corey?" He changed the subject.

"I'm in marketing."

"Corey works for your father now," Terry added, motioning to Clara. "He started shortly after you left."

Clara's eyes turned to him before smiling over at Corey. "Congrats on the job. I hope you like working at Sunset Dreams."

"I do." He nodded. "I had hoped to tell you… myself." Corey shifted in his seat.

Holly waved him off. "There are loads of people working for Sunset Dreams now. I mean, it is one of the biggest realty firms in California." She dismissed the conversation and turned to him. "What is it you do, Reagan?"

"Please don't tell me you're in real estate like your family," Emily groaned.

"No," he agreed. "I'm in the private sector now." He knew that didn't tell them anything, but he hadn't thought through this part of approaching the group.

"As in, you used to work for the military?" Corey asked.

"You certainly look the military type," Emily said, running her eyes over him. He'd had enough women look at him like that over the years.

"Reagan runs a personal security firm," Clara jumped in, squeezing his hand. He instantly liked the sound of it. After all, he was acting as her personal security.

lara could tell Reagan was struggling with coming up with how to explain what he did without giving too much away.

"How exciting," Holly added before the next round of drinks were delivered.

The conversation turned away from work and towards the past five years. She again was asked why they were in town, this time by Corey. She made sure to mention they were there to sell her stocks in her father's business. Corey shocked her by adding that he'd buy them from her.

"I don't think you understand," Holly chuckled. "For her eighteenth birthday, her dad gave her a tenth of the business."

"A..." Corey's chin dropped. "Holy hell, that means..." He whistled. "That's too rich for my blood." He sighed and leaned back. "I guess I should have proposed when I had the chance."

Terry elbowed him in the ribs and then leaned forward. "You know, my dad mentioned something about wanting to get his hands on more stocks. I bet he'd buy them from you."

This time it was Reagan that leaned forward. "Maybe you can pass it along to him? What do you think, baby?" He turned to her. "Do you want him to meet us at the hotel to discuss it?"

"Sure," she answered, seeing the eagerness in his eyes.

Not that they were really going to sell her shares, since her father technically still had a hold on them, but if they really did have something to do with her sister's death, they were the bait.

"I'll let him know." Terry waved the conversation off. "Now, how about a toast…"

The rest of the night ground on like a bad dream. In the past five years, she'd never once thought about hanging out with this group of people again. She'd burned that bridge. No, more accurately, they had. This part of her life was gone. It had died with Gina.

Almost an hour later, her phone pinged with a message and she pulled it out.

-Want to leave?

It was from Reagan. She hadn't even seen him pull out his phone.

-God yes!

She replied quickly. Glancing down at his watch, he read her reply on its face, and smiled. Then, without missing a beat, he stood.

"Ready?" He held out his hand. "It was nice meeting everyone." He helped her stand. "We'd like to stay, but we've got dinner arrangements," he told the group smoothly.

"How long did you say you'd be back in town?" Terry

asked.

"We're not sure. Hopefully, just until I can unload my stocks," she answered as Reagan wrapped his arm around her waist.

"Call us, we'll get together again before you go," Emily added easily.

"Don't go disappearing again on us," Holly added with a sad look. "I mean it."

"I won't," she promised her. "Night," she said and followed Reagan out of the crowded building.

"So?" he asked once they were in the rental car.

"Seeing them all together was a shock." She rested her head back. "I hadn't planned for it."

"It was kind of a good thing, though. We did get a little information from the ordeal, thanks to your ex."

"Oh?" She turned her head towards Reagan.

"We got further confirmation that Henry Knight was looking to pick up some extra stocks in your father's business," he added as he pulled out of the parking garage.

"It's a smart move." She sighed and watched the city lights pass outside her window. "My father's company is the largest in California."

"Was," he added. "In the past few years, things have taken a dive," he responded, shocking her.

"What?" She sat up a little.

"Don't get me wrong. It's still worth millions. But the stocks have taken a steady slide ever since Gina's death. Some claim it's because your father has stepped aside while others blame Henry Knight's reckless hold on the company while your father is handling family issues."

"That would be me, the murdering daughter." She tensed and closed her eyes to block out all of the hurtful things her father had said earlier. "My father's family issue."

"No." He reached over and took her hand, then raised it to his lips. "They only mention the death of Gina."

She nodded and relaxed again. "What now?" she asked again. Thanks to the four drinks, her head was swimming.

Even though they had spent the majority of yesterday in bed, she had gotten little sleep.

"Now, we wait. We'll set up a meeting with Henry Knight and see where that leads us."

"He might know that I don't really have my hands on my shares or that I co-own them with my father," she mentioned.

"Something tells me that it won't matter," he said as they pulled into the parking garage for the hotel.

"No," she agreed. If her sister had been killed because of the shares, which she hadn't even had in her possession yet, then whoever had hired the man who had attacked Reagan in Florida wouldn't stop until they got control of hers.

Reagan spent a few minutes on the phone while Clara showered the next morning. He made a few calls to his father, who had talked with the family lawyer about Clara's next steps legally with her family.

She'd mentioned over and over that she didn't want any of her father's money. However, he'd suggested that if she didn't get it there was a possibility that the killer would get it all.

"You think it's Rebecca?" she asked, sounding

shocked.

"She's on my list of suspects," he said smoothly.

Her hands went to her hips. "Maybe we should go over that list."

He held up his hand, fingers out as he ticked them off.

"Your father, your stepmother, Henry Knight, and after last night, Corey Wells."

"Okay."

He could tell that she was offended that her father and stepmother were on his list, but she promised him that she would think about everything from an outsider's perspective.

After getting off the phone with his father, he sent a text message to his sister. When they left California, he was planning on making a stop in Arizona since he'd missed her during her visit home.

"Is everything okay?" Clara asked from the bathroom doorway.

"Yeah, just telling my little sister we might stop by when we leave here." He walked over and wrapped her in his arms. She'd wrapped a towel around her body, and her hair was still dripping wet. She looked even better than when she'd worn the sexy blue number the night before.

"I could get used to this." She sighed as she leaned into him. "Just you and me. No interruptions." She rested her head against his chest. Just then, her cell phone rang.

He chuckled. "You cursed it."

She stepped away and glanced down at her phone.

"It's Terry's father," she said, looking down at her screen. "He's coming back into town this morning and wants to meet at his office." She glanced up at him. "He must not know about the joint shares."

"We'll find out when we get there," Reagan supplied. "What time?"

She glanced back down at her phone. "In an hour. You're going with me?"

"I'm not letting you walk into that building alone." He moved closer to her again before kissing her.

Just under an hour later, they walked into the Sunset Dreams building. It wasn't the tallest or biggest building downtown, but it was still very impressive.

During his visit the other day, he'd found out that they did everything from selling and purchasing to investments and more. He found it all quite interesting. After all he had family in real estate. His uncle Luke now owned his family's business, Crystal Resorts, which had more than a dozen buildings along the Panhandle. Not to mention, his uncles still ran Paradise Construction.

"Knight's office is on the top floor," he said, remembering Rebecca Cruz's visit. "Does your stepmother do any work down here?" he asked once they were alone in the elevator.

"No." She shook her head. "Rebecca never liked coming down here. This is all...too far beneath her. I've always liked her, but looking back now, I realize just how shallow she is."

They stepped out of the elevators into a reception area.

"Clara Cruz and Reagan Grayton to see Mr. Knight," he told the woman. Upon hearing Clara's name, the woman jumped up.

"Yes, of course, Miss Cruz." The fact that the woman ignored him completely told him that she knew exactly who was visiting her boss.

She showed them down a hallway filled with small

offices. When they reached the large corner one, she knocked on the door and opened it slightly. "Miss Cruz to see you."

"Send her in," he heard a deep voice bellow out.

The woman swung open the door to reveal a massive office. There was glass from ceiling to floor, showcasing a beautiful view of the city and the Hollywood Hills in the distance.

"Clara." Henry rushed around the neatly organized glass desk. The man was nothing like he'd expected. He'd expected a man who looked similar to Terry: tall, tan, toned. Instead, Henry Knight was short and extremely pudgy. Not that he wasn't in shape. He moved quickly and confidently, and that told Reagan a lot. There were golf clubs tucked into the corner of the room that looked like they hadn't been used in years. Yet there were pictures of a younger version of him on the golf course with Clara's father and other groups of men.

"Henry, this is Reagan Grayton." Clara introduced him after she was free of the older man's hug.

"Nice to meet you." He held out a hand and it was instantly taken into a warm handshake.

"When Terry told me you were home…" The man smiled and patted his heart. "Well, let's just say this old ticker skipped a few beats for joy."

Clara chuckled. "How are you?" she asked as he motioned for them to sit down.

"I'm…" The man's smile and steps faltered. "Doing good."

Reagan could tell that the man was lying. As he sat down, the man shoved a stack of medical bills into a drawer and closed it.

Clara seemed ignorant to the fact and continued on. "I happened to mention to Terry last night that I was thinking of selling my shares in the business."

"Yes." He frowned. "Does your father know?"

"My shares were gifted to me on my eighteenth birthday."

"Yes, I remember. I was at the party." He smiled easily. "But I would have thought that you'd offer them up to your father first?"

"My father has made his stance very clear on... the past." She swallowed. They had planned how to handle the questions. "I can't stick around here anymore." She looked around the building as if even this office brought up bad memories. "I want to start over." She reached for his hand. "Somewhere new. The shares are tying me down. My father doesn't want me to sell them."

"I understand." Henry nodded. "Of course, I'd be happy to take them off your hands. Unfortunately, they aren't worth what they used to be."

"Oh?" she asked. Their plan to get information directly from the horse's mouth seemed to be working.

"In the past few years... Since Gina's death, your father has had a lack of interest in the business and it has shown. Share prices have slumped."

"Is the business in trouble?" she asked.

"No." He shook his head. "It hasn't come to anything... drastic, but I thought I ought to warn you."

"I see." She nodded. "Is there anything I can do?"

"No." The older man sighed. "Short of a miracle or getting your father to show interest in his business again, nothing."

CHAPTER 17

Clara listened to Henry say that he'd have his lawyers contact theirs and then they said their goodbyes.

After leaving the office, Reagan took her arm and started walking slowly down the hallway.

"He's ill," he said under his breath.

"He…" She jerked and glanced back over her shoulder. "How do you know?"

"Medical bills. His desk was filled with them when we walked in. I'm guessing the last week he was off for personal reasons was really due to something medical. How does he look?"

Before she could answer, an office door opened and Corey stepped out, almost bumping into her and toppling her over. Thankfully, Reagan was there and steadied her.

"Clara?" He frowned when he noticed who he had almost bumped over.

"Corey." She smiled, remembering that he'd

mentioned he worked there now. "Is this your office?" She glanced into the room.

"Yeah." He shut the door as he shifted the stacks of papers in his hands. "I'm sorry, I would chat, but I'm running late for a meeting." He nodded towards Henry's office. "If you have time, let's meet up later?" His eyes moved over to Reagan.

"Sure," she said easily.

Out of all of her friends, Corey was the only one who had contacted her after Gina's death. Her father had turned him away at the door, claiming that she needed her rest, but at least he'd tried.

She hadn't even had the guts to break up with him before running away. She'd always felt bad about leaving things the way she had, but she'd needed her life to change and thought he would understand.

Reagan didn't speak again until they were back in the car. "Do you think he'll tell your father?" he asked.

Since her mind was still on Corey, she asked, "Who?"

"Knight?" He pulled out of the parking garage. "Do you think he'll tell your father that you're trying to sell the shares?"

"Oh, I don't know." She shifted in the seat, ready for some lunch already. "He might. They were always close."

"Then we'd better get there first," he answered. "How do you feel about lunch?"

"I'd love some, but how does that get us talking to my father first?"

He chuckled. "He's having lunch at the country club. I saw his name on the registration the other day when you were there."

Her eyes narrowed. "You're like a super spy," she accused, causing him to chuckle.

"Grayton… Reagan Grayton." He frowned. "Not as good as Bond, but it'll do." He smiled.

Thankfully, her name was still technically on the guest list for the club, and they were seated at a table in the main dining hall. She knew her father always liked this room better than sitting outside or by the pool, so the chances of them seeing him were high.

They had just ordered when Reagan touched her arm. "He's here," he said softly. "And sees us."

She was a little surprised to see her father walking across the room towards them alone. She'd expected Rebecca to be with him, since they usually lunched together at the club.

"Dad," she said easily, picking up her wine glass. "Care to join us?"

"What are you two doing here?" he asked, glancing around the room as if he was embarrassed to be seen talking with her.

"Celebrating. We've just agreed to sell my shares in Sunset Dreams." Her father's face paled.

"You…" he sputtered. "You can't." He shook his head again and sat down hard in the chair across from her. There had been a time when she would have instantly worried about his health. But not anymore. If he really did believe she had murdered Gina, so much so that he'd removed her from his will, then she had to stop caring what he did. Still, it weighed on her, seeing him like that.

"Clara, you're making a big mistake pursuing this. The shares are in both of our names. You need my approval to sell them." Her father took her hand and leaned closer to whisper to her. "Besides, you don't want to get yourself tied up in this mess. Please." He turned to Reagan. "While you can, take her away from here." He glanced around again. "Go, before it's..." He stopped talking when Rebecca and Henry Knight walked into the room. "He called us and wanted to meet for lunch," he added quickly.

"Why, Carlo, what's wrong?" Rebecca rushed to his side. Worry marred her face. "Was it something Clara said?" Her eyes narrowed in her direction.

"No, darling, I'm just hungry." Her father stood up and rubbed his belly. "Clara was just telling me about your meeting," her father added. "We can discuss the details later," he told Henry. Clara got the feeling that a secret message had passed between the men.

"Good, enough talk about business," Henry added, taking Rebecca's arm. "How about we go and enjoy our lunch?" He started walking her towards their waiting table.

Her father turned and quietly said, "This is for your own good."

~

"You don't think..." Clara said the moment they were back in their hotel room.

"What?" he asked when she didn't finish her question.

She turned to him after tossing her purse on the sofa. "You don't think my dad is playing a game with us, do you? That he's pretending?"

"Pretending what?"

"I don't know." She threw up her hands in frustration. "It just doesn't make sense."

"What doesn't?" He sat down on the edge of the bed.

"Any of it." She walked over to the windows to look out at the view. Then she suddenly turned back. "Him pulling me out of his will. He paid you to find me, then acts like I'm the murderer." She shook her head. "Before I ran away, Dad was the only one who told me he believed in me." She crossed her arms over her chest and closed her eyes. "I believed him back then."

"Okay," he said slowly. Then her eyes opened and met his.

"I don't believe him now when he acts like I killed Gina. Something has changed."

"He acted afraid when you told him about selling the shares," Reagan recalled. At first, he'd believed the man had been angry, but after hearing him warn them off, his opinion had changed.

"Yes." She pointed at him. "Exactly."

"So, then the question is… why?" He pulled his laptop from the hotel safe and set it on the desk so they could research how much Sunset Dreams Realty shares were worth and, more important, why.

Two hours later, Clara rested on the bed while Reagan ordered room service. The fancy club they had eaten at served small portions for high prices.

After ordering a burger with fries and two milkshakes, he continued to search for any information he could on her father's business.

Just before the food arrived, he changed his tactics and started looking into Henry Knight's health issues.

"I found something," he said, waking Clara up. "Sorry." He glanced over at her just as a knock on the door sounded. "That will be the room service." He got up to get the door.

Coming back in with the tray, he set it down and lifted the lid. "I got you a shake. I figured we could share the burger and fries."

"The shake is fine for me." She took it from him. "Maybe a few fries." She snagged a few off his plate as she looked over his shoulder at the screen. "What did you find?"

"Henry Knight isn't the one who's sick," he said with confidence.

"He isn't?"

"No." He pulled up the image of the man helping his daughter Terry into a car after a controversial surgery in Europe.

"Terry?" She sat down next to him. "What?" Her eyes scanned the page. "That's why she didn't want to be left alone with me." She closed her eyes. "She didn't want to tell me she was dying."

"Not yet. It says in the article that this picture was taken over a year ago. Her cancer is in remission."

"So, Henry racks up the medical bills for Terry, paying for a treatment that saves her, only to, what? Kill Gina for her shares because he can't pay for it all? I don't buy it." She shook her head. "Besides, there is no way Terry was sick back when Gina was killed five years ago."

Reagan's shoulders slumped. "Right." He shut down his computer. "Okay, so if not Henry, then… who?"

CHAPTER 18

That question played in Clara's mind all night long. Who? Who would have wanted her sister dead five years ago? And why?

If only Clara could remember more from that day. But every time she tried to remember; all she came up with was blackness.

"What do you think of hypnosis?" she asked Reagan a few days later.

They had been keeping a low profile while they continued to search for more clues. Since she had no desire to be in California, she kept to the hotel. Most of their meals were ordered through room service.

Even though she found herself bored, being in the same room with him was still better than venturing out alone.

"I've never tried it," he admitted as he turned towards her.

She'd been watching an episode of CSI about two women being hypnotized.

"You're thinking of trying to remember that night?" he asked.

"That entire day. Maybe the reason I can't remember anything is because I saw or did something that would shed light on what happened." She sat up. "I've often wondered why they murdered Gina and not me? I mean, if you're going to kill one of us, why not both?"

"They needed to frame you," he said smoothly. "Once you were locked up for the crime…"—he motioned with his hand— "they would be in the clear to do…whatever they had planned."

"Then why wait five years? I mean, if their move is to drive down my father's business… I just don't see any profit to it."

He snapped his fingers and pulled out his phone, putting it on speaker.

"Hey, Uncle Luke, I'm here with Clara. Can you tell her what happened to your family's business shares after your dad had his stroke?"

"Hey." Clara heard his uncle's cheery voice. "Sure. I took over for my dad. The share prices took a huge dive because I was, and I'm quoting this, 'Unstable for the business.'"

"Then what?" Reagan asked. "What happened after that?"

"Well, I shocked them all by buying up the discarded shares they didn't want." She could hear humor in Luke's voice.

"Then what?" Reagan smiled as they waited.

"Well, about three months later, I shocked them again by buying a sketchy property, a purchase that went against my father's better judgment when he was alive. He'd been after Cassey's place. She wasn't selling, so I bought a different plot of land for a lot less than what we would have paid for her place on the boardwalk. We made millions after the share prices skyrocketed due to the new family friendly hotel I built on the location. When the dust cleared, I owned the majority of the shares in the company and they were easily worth triple what I had purchased them for."

Reagan looked at her. "Thanks."

"Any time," Luke added cheerfully. "You think this has something to do with Clara's sister and her father's business?"

"We'll let you know," he said before saying his goodbyes.

"So." She waited. "You think someone killed my sister to get her shares so they could drive down the price of them. And then what? Buy more? Then build them back up?"

"It's a long shot, but it could happen. It has happened lots of times before. I wouldn't put it past someone to murder someone, especially if we're talking millions. You said you received a tenth of the business?" he asked.

When she nodded, he turned back around and asked over his shoulder. "Was your dad going to give Gina the same amount?"

"I think so." She shrugged. "We didn't really, you know, care or know what it meant at the time. Only that it was a gift that meant a lot to our father."

"So, if this is the case, who stands to gain the most from it?" He turned back around and asked her. "Currently, your tenth of the shares in the business are worth ten point three million."

"What?" she gasped. She was thankful she was sitting down. She'd never even imagined her father's business was worth that much.

"Trust me when I say, that's nothing compared to what they could be worth. When your father gifted them to you…" He turned around and calculated again. "They were worth almost double that."

She swallowed and closed her eyes. "My god." She felt her stomach roll. "I…" She shook her head then jumped up from the bed and rushed to the bathroom, where she threw up, making it to the toilet just in time.

"Hey." Reagan was right there behind her. "It's okay." He rubbed her back.

"Go away. I don't want…" She was sick again. "Please," she cried as he handed her a towel and a glass of water.

"Sip it," he warned.

"I don't want you to see me." She groaned as she buried her head in the towel. "Please, I'm so…"

"Embarrassed?" She could hear the frown in his tone. "Don't be. Everyone gets sick. I had to help Bella each time she got sick. My mother hasn't the stomach for it." He chuckled. "I would have ended up cleaning up after both of them."

She rested her back against the bathroom wall. "No wonder someone murdered Gina and framed me." She closed her eyes on the pain. "All of that money."

"Millions," he agreed. "Tens of millions, which could easily jump back up to hundreds of millions, if your father stepped back in and ran the business."

Again, her stomach rolled. "Rebecca?" she said under her breath.

"We need to find out why your dad is still at home," he said softly. "How about you clean up. I'll order us some food and we can rest tonight.

"No." She shook her head. "I don't want to wait any longer." She walked over and started to brush her teeth. "It has to be tonight," she said with the toothbrush still in her mouth. "I'm tired of waiting. She's gotten away with this for too long."

Reagan stood beside her as she rang the doorbell. She'd freshened up after being sick and then had called her father, telling him only that they needed to talk.

Rebecca opened the door again. This time, there wasn't a hug or a squeal.

"Come on in." She motioned for them to enter. They followed her back to where Clara's father was sitting in the living room, waiting for them.

"Dad." She nodded and sat across from him.

"This sounded urgent," he said, looking a little worried.

"It is." Clara glanced over at Rebecca.

"I can get some drinks." She started to leave.

"No." Clara stopped her. "Sit, this involves you."

Rebecca's perfectly manicured eyebrows rose slightly. "Oh?" She tilted her head but made no move to sit down.

"Yes, why don't you have a seat?" Clara nodded to the spot next to her father.

Rebecca moved slowly but finally sat down across from them.

"You aren't pregnant, are you?" Rebecca gasped after a moment.

"No." Clara frowned and shook her head slightly, then she glanced over at him. The look in her eyes let him know that she was unsure of what to do next.

"Mr. Cruz, we think that your daughter, that Gina, was murdered for the ten percent shares in your business you were going to give her," he said quickly.

Rebecca gasped again and covered her heart with her hands. "No." She shook her head. "Oh, my poor baby."

The fact that Clara's father remained silent told him that the man had already guessed as much.

"But…" Clara's stepmother turned to her father. "Honey, don't those have to be in someone's name? You were going to do joint shares again. Even if they did kill Gina for her shares, you would have to sign them over, correct?"

"Yes," Carlo said softly. "I would." He nodded, avoiding Clara's eyes.

"Well, there you have it then." Rebecca started to stand up. "I'll just go get those drinks then."

"They wouldn't have to sell them, not if they inherited them after their husband died and left everything in his will to them, including the shares."

Rebecca froze mid-step. Slowly, she turned around. "Are you… accusing me of murdering my own daughter?"

"Step," Clara added quickly. Her eyes narrowed as they both watched Rebecca's face for any hint of guilt.

"This is preposterous." Rebecca rushed back over to Carlo's side. "I loved that girl like she was my own. Both of you." She motioned to Clara. "I have everything I could ever want here. Why would I jeopardize what I have?" She turned to her husband. "Tell them." She waved her arms around the room.

Instead of answering, Carlo glanced up at her. "I've had my doubts over the years myself," he said softly, shocking everyone in the room except Reagan.

CHAPTER 19

Clara stood up, breaking the silence. "I can't remember anything from that day. I have a list of medications here." She pulled the list Reagan had printed at the hotel out of her pocket. "Medications that can cause someone memory loss. If I go up to your bathroom, would I find any of those in your cupboard still? Would any of these be on a list your doctor prescribed to you back then?"

Rebecca's eyes narrowed. "No, I don't take any pills." She waved the accusation off.

"No, but I do." Her father stood up. "And you have access to them." He held out his hands and she handed the list to him.

"I can see two so far that I have somewhere in the house."

"We all know you were lying about the memory loss." Rebecca's voice rose. "You didn't even tell the police about it," she accused.

"I was young and had just woken up next to my

murdered sister." Clara heard her voice crack and tightened her fist to hold back the slew of emotions that were bubbling to get out. "I'd never been arrested or questioned by the police before," she said a little more calmly.

"You were covered in Gina's blood."

"Because I woke on the floor, next to her. As if I'd just passed out after finding her like that. Even the medical examiner claimed that I had no defensive wounds. That the blood on my hands could have come about because I'd tried to stop Gina from bleeding out."

That seemed to stump her stepmother. Her eyes were darting back and forth between her and her father.

Then, suddenly, she calmed down. "Lies." She smiled. "You have no proof. It's been five years. Don't you think I would have made a move on Carlo's life by now if I was after his money?"

"You couldn't." Her father turned to her. "At least not until I officially change my will. Which you constantly asked me to for the past five years and which I finally told you I had just recently, however..." Her father turned and looked at Rebecca. "I lied. I never changed my will."

A high pitch sound started deep in Rebecca's chest. "You lied?" she cried out. "You lied about changing your will?"

"Yes," her father said easily as he raised his chin. "I was hoping it wasn't you, but I noticed how you had reacted to Clara's return. The moment she came back, you started building up the lies, telling me how smart it was for me to cut her from the will. You had a million reasons for keeping the money from her. It was hard to convince me to cut her from my will when she wasn't around, but the second she stepped foot back into this house, you had a list going."

"I won't stand here and listen to these lies." She started to move towards the door, but Reagan stepped in front of the hallway.

"You're not going anywhere. Not until the police get here and we go over this all once more with them," Reagan said, pulling out his cell phone.

"This is my house—"

"Sit down," her father yelled across the room. "This is *my* house. Your name isn't even on the title," he growled. "Nor is it ever going to be. When I go, everything I have still goes to Clara." He nodded to her.

When Rebecca stayed where she was, Regan motioned to the chair as he dialed the phone.

"What I don't get is," Clara said softly, "who did Gina scratch? You were the one to find me and Gina." She noticed the look in her stepmother's eyes as they darted towards the hallway.

To her horror and surprise, she noticed Corey standing just outside of her father's office. He held a gun in his hands, pointed directly at Reagan's chest as he dialed the police.

"Reagan!" she screamed, just as Corey pulled the trigger.

Out of the corner of her eye, she saw Reagan hit the ground. He landed behind one of the white sofas. Then she was being tossed to the ground by her father as another shot rang out in the room.

With the weight of her father pinning her down, she gasped for air and tried to free herself so she could find out if Reagan was alive.

She continued to cry for him until a shadow fell over her. Looking up into Corey's face, she remembered a time when she'd imagined him to be attractive. Back when she'd dated men that she believed would give her everything she'd wanted in life.

"Corey?" She shook her head. "Why?"

Rebecca walked over and wrapped her arms around her ex-boyfriend.

"Your sister found out about us." He motioned with his free hand between him and Rebecca. "We wanted to get some of your father's money but after what happened that night, we made a new plan to get all of it. Including the shares, we hadn't even really care about those before, but with our new plan we could have had it all. That night changed everything, when Gina walked in on us. It was stupid of us to steal a moment alone, but... when you're in love... Gina was very upset and threatened to expose us right there during her party. You see, I was all set to propose to you that night. That way, we would have been able to continue to see each other behind your back while enjoying the lifestyle we wanted. Then, once your old man died, we could finally be together. Instead, we came up with a plan to frame you so that Rebecca could convince Carlo to remove you from his will while you took the fall and rotted away in jail. I spent the next week hiding while my arms healed from Gina's attack. But then you took off on us. Rebecca tried to convince Carlo that you were guilty, but without you around, he wouldn't listen. You ruined everything by taking off on us," he screamed. But then he smiled. "But then your father hired him." He motioned with his free hand to the other side of the room where Reagan was. "Rebecca filled me in on his reports, and I flew down to Florida and hired some bum off the street to kill you and make it look like a robbery." He shrugged and she remembered that first night someone had attacked her. "You know what they say—never hire a crack addict to do a job you want done right."

"You shot Reagan?" she asked, remembering the second night.

"Yeah, but then I heard sirens." He sighed. "And got spooked."

"What about Reagan's car accident?" She asked, unsure of why they would go after him.

"A moment of sheer stupidity." He shrugged. "I thought for a moment that if I got rid of him, it would convince your father you were trying to hide something; besides, I hated the way the guy looked at you." He turned towards Rebecca. "And the way she looked at him."

Clara's eyes were glued to the gun pointing at her forehead. She wanted to look away to see if Reagan was okay, but she was frozen in place with fear.

"Baby, it's only ever been you." Rebecca jumped in. "We didn't mean to kill her," Rebecca added. "She jumped at Corey and scratched him," she added, holding onto the younger man. "I… I just picked up the first thing near me and…" The woman closed her eyes. "I really did love you girls like you were mine." She sniffled. But the fact that her body was pressed up against Corey's as he pointed a gun at her head didn't convince Clara that she was sincere. "Corey snuck some of your father's pills into your drink and we moved you in to the office, then… I waited and found you after I heard you scream for help."

Just then she heard her father groan and the gun was quickly turned to aim at him instead. Clara swung out her legs, catching Corey in the shins. The gun went flying out of his hands as he fell backwards.

She pushed her father aside and scrambled for the weapon just as Rebecca flung herself on top of her. Then she was fighting her stepmother, the woman who had helped raise her, for her life.

~

"Son of a..." Reagan cursed under his breath when he woke and felt the sting of yet another bullet that had ripped through his skin. Instantly, he jerked back to the now and remembered Clara.

Glancing around, he heard someone fighting and pushed off the ground. Finding his phone, he finished dialing nine-one-one. Then he chanced a glance around the sofa and saw Rebecca and Clara wrestling for the gun. Corey was kneeling on the ground, holding a large gash on his forehead.

He heard Clara scream and dropped his phone to rush to help her. He hoisted Rebecca off of Clara, and the woman kicked out and screamed as he tossed her through the air.

This gave Clara access to the gun, which she then turned on him blindly.

"Easy, baby, I've already taken two bullets for you. I'm thinking my luck is going to run out if I take another one." He held up his hands towards her.

"Reagan," she cried out, jumping into his arms. "They... they killed Gina," she cried against his chest.

"Easy," he said, taking the gun from her hands and holding it out so that Rebecca didn't run out of the house.

"Baby," he said to Clara, "my phone. Tell the dispatcher the address." He motioned with his free hand.

She ran over and picked up the phone, then rushed to her father's side. "Daddy?" she cried, then she relayed the information over the phone.

"He's just hit his head," she said after a moment. "No, he's breathing normally. Daddy?" she said again.

He watched out of the corner of his eye as her father started to come to. A groan from Corey had him stepping back. "Tell them we have wounded," he added, feeling the spot on his wrist starting to sting. Switching the gun to his left hand, he glanced down at the spot. "Damn," he said. "Clara." He glanced down at her. When she noticed the gouge out of his skin, she cried out, dropping the phone and rushing to his side.

"You've been shot." She wrapped his wrist in a throw blanket. Tying it off as tight as she could, she applied pressure.

"I did tell you I'd taken two bullets for you." He smiled. "I'm okay, I just think maybe you should..." He handed her the gun. "I need to sit for a moment. This time it hurts a lot worse, and I don't want to pass out and have these two idiots rush you."

He moved over and sat on the edge of the opposite sofa. His eyes were still glued to Rebecca, and he occasionally glanced over at Corey, who was still moaning on the floor as more blood spurted from the gash.

"How did he get hurt?" he asked Clara.

"I kicked him," she answered proudly. "He hit his head on the corner of the glass coffee table." Then she turned to her stepmother. "You're awfully quiet." She smiled. "Trying to figure out how you're going to get out of this?"

"You have no proof. It's your word against ours," she started, but Reagan's chuckling stopped her.

"We came in fully prepared to get a confession." He nodded to the phone lying next to her father. "The recording should be enough evidence. That and I'd expect Corey's DNA matches that found under Gina's nails. I'm betting he's never done a 23andMe test before since he wasn't in the database."

He knew he was mumbling but talking made him focus on something other than the fact that his wrist bone was most likely broken and half of the skin covering the bone was gone.

"Reagan?" Clara's soft voice anchored him even further.

"Talk to me, baby," he said softly. "I need to stay awake."

Just then, her father sat up. "Clara?" he asked, looking around.

"Daddy, help Reagan. He's been shot," she said, keeping her eyes on Corey as he started to move as well.

Just then, he could hear the sirens in the distance and relaxed slightly.

"You okay?" Carlo asked as he glanced down at the blood-soaked blanket.

"I'm going to marry your daughter," he said, "and I'll be pretty pissed if you try to stop me." Then he passed out cold.

CHAPTER 20

Over the next three days, Clara spent as much time as she could in Reagan's hospital room. He'd had two surgeries, the first one to put pins in his broken bone, the second to patch the chunk of skin that was missing with a piece from just above his hip. Each time he went under the knife, she worried.

His parents arrived the morning after the shooting and had spent as much time with him as she had. The second day, his sister Bella showed up.

Clara had instantly liked the younger girl. Even though she was only five years younger than her, Bella informed her that she was graduating college later that year.

"How young were you when you started?" she asked, impressed.

"I graduated high school at sixteen." She smiled.

"Both of our kids did. Reagan was so bored during school, the only way to get him to sit still in class was to give him more challenging work," Marissa added with pride in her eyes.

"They take after me," Roman added with a wink.

"Right," Marissa and Bella said at the same time.

"It took you seven years to find Mom and Reagan, who were living less than fifty miles from you."

"Smart aleck." Roman hugged his daughter.

Clara thought about her family. She'd always believed she had taken after her father, until one day she'd seen a picture of her mother. Both Gina and she had taken after Ronda Cruz, a woman who had died far too young.

The day they released Reagan, they spent the night back at the hotel, since she couldn't walk into her father's house without the memories surfacing.

She was surprised when her father showed up at their hotel room.

"I thought I'd come see how Reagan was doing," he said as she let him into the suite. Reagan's parents had taken the other room so they could be close to him. They all had tickets to fly back to Florida the following day, and they had wanted to remain close to Reagan.

"He's doing fine." She motioned to where Reagan sat on the sofa, his right arm resting on the side of the sofa while he tried to eat a plate of spaghetti with his left hand.

"Carlo, come on in," Reagan called out.

"He's on pain pills," she explained quietly. She'd tried to get him to swallow the pills the doctor had prescribed him, but he'd refused. Until his mother stepped into the room and gave him a look. Then he'd swallowed them without complaints.

"You'll have to show me how you do that," she'd murmured to her.

"I didn't get a chance to say thank you." Her father sat next to Reagan. "For saving my daughter."

Reagan smiled and set his fork down. When his plate teetered on the edge of the sofa, she moved it quickly before it ended up on the floor.

"I love her. I'll take a million bullets for her if I have to." He smiled. "You hurt her." He frowned. "She thought… that you believed she'd killed Gina."

"Never," her father said, his eyes turning to hers. "I knew something was up. Henry and I… we both knew it. We thought we could draw Rebecca and her co-conspirator out ourselves. I never wanted you to get hurt. Either of you." He glanced between them both. "I needed Rebecca to think that I had changed my will so that I was the target and not you."

"Dad." She rested her hand on his shoulder.

"I never meant to hurt you. Really." He stood up and wrapped her in his arms. "I love you. I loved your sister so much."

His body shook and she realized he was crying. She held onto him more tightly and joined him.

When he pulled back, he shocked her by adding, "They're looking into Ronda's death. The police." He wiped his eyes with a tissue Reagan's mother handed him. She took the one she offered to her as well.

"What?" she balked. "Mom?" She shook her head.

"Rebecca mentioned something about it when she was interviewed. They think there's a possibility that she poisoned Ronda." He buried his face in his hands. "She killed your mother to get closer to me and all for money. I was so blind. I should have never allowed myself to trust someone else. You girls were everything to me, at one point. Then… I wish I'd never started my business. I lost sight of what was important to me. I allowed my greed and the new power I had to blind me." He looked up at her, his eyes red from tears. "How can you ever forgive me? Your mother and sister are gone because… I trusted someone I shouldn't have."

"Dad." She held him again. What could she say? She'd never been as happy as when she'd been scraping pennies to pay bills. When she'd had access to anything and everything, she'd been blind to real friendships and had taken her family for granted.

"I was blinded too. She fooled us all. We can start again," she suggested. "California is the old us. Come with us to Florida. Let the past die here." She leaned back and looked into her dad's eyes. "Let's start over together."

He nodded. "I haven't been able to go back to the house." He closed his eyes as more tears slid down his face. "I haven't even gotten any clothes. Henry had to send Terry over there to pack a bag for me. I'm staying just down the hallway." She smiled and motioned for him to sit down again. "Then let's order you some room service so you can eat with the family. Your new family." She glanced over at Reagan. "Since we're going to be married."

"We are?" Reagan asked, reaching for his pasta again.

"As soon as you sober up and get around to asking me." She said with a laugh.

Reagan stood in the soft sugar sands of the Gulf of Mexico and held onto Clara. His family and her dad were all enjoying the warm water just a few feet away from them. It had been two months since they returned to Florida.

Two long months of healing both physically and mentally.

The beach was filled with laughter and love. He knew this was the right moment and pulled the small box from his back pocket.

"Is it time?" she asked, smiling up at him.

"You knew this was coming." He laughed. "From the moment I walked into Rico's, we both did." He opened the box. "So, are you going to take this? Or do I have to take another bullet first?"

She reached over and slipped the ring out of the black box, then slid it onto her finger. "Let me hear you say it one more time." She looked up at him with her dark eyes.

"Marry me," he said easily.

"No, the other thing." She shook her head.

"I love you." He pulled her closer.

"When are we going to make it official?" she asked, wrapping her arms around his shoulders.

"Soon, today, tomorrow, whenever you want. As long as it's soon."

"Good, because I'd hate to have to buy a maternity wedding dress," she said, frowning down as she covered her flat belly.

"A…" He frowned. "You're…" He didn't wait for her to answer. Instead he picked her up and spun her around the beach. Then he carted her into the waters and told their family that there was going to be one more Grayton.

"Make that two," he added after she showed off the ring that he'd picked out for her. When her hands went to her belly, everyone cheered and hugged them both again.

That evening, sitting in front of the bonfire, he held

onto Clara and whispered in her ear, "I've never been so happy in my life." He kissed the spot.

"Neither have I." She sighed. "You know, I think your aunt likes my father." She motioned to where her dad was flirting with his aunt Julie.

"I've never seen aunt Julie act like that before." He chuckled. "There has to be at least twenty years between them." He frowned over as her father moved a strand of his aunt's hair out of her eyes.

"Relax," Clara laughed. "I think it's sweet. Besides, my father is closer to her age then he was with Rebecca."

"I'm not worried about him. After all, Julie is the one who's older."

Clara chuckled and turned in his arms. "Love has no boundaries." She kissed him. "For the first time in his life, I don't think he's worrying if she's after him for his money."

"No," he agreed. "Julie isn't that kind of person." He relaxed a little. "Besides, all my life she's never been with anyone before." He frowned. "Actually, I don't think she's ever been with anyone. She's always been just... Aunt Julie." He shrugged.

"Then she deserves to be happy. Let's not spoil it. If it's meant to be..." She relaxed back in his arms. "Now, talk to me about weddings and babies." She stilled and glanced over her shoulder. "Where are we going to live?"

He pulled her close. "I've been house hunting, but my uncle Marcus has promised me that if I find a lot of land, he'll build us our dream home."

She sighed. "I like that idea. Making something of our own." She rested her hand over her belly, and he covered her hand with his good one, since his right hand was still in a sling.

"I hope it's a girl," he said out of the blue. "We can call her Gina, after the aunt that brought us together." He kissed the top of her head, but she flung herself around and held onto him.

"I love you," she said against his lips. "So much."

"I'm never going to let you go. I promise every day from here on out is going to be better than this one."

She laughed. "Then I'm never going to let you go, either."

"That's a deal I'll take," he said before kissing her again.

DIGITAL ISBN: 978-1-945100-04-8

PRINT ISBN: 978-1-098688-65-3

Copyeditor: Erica Ellis – inkdeepediting.com

The Pride Series

Finding Pride

Discovering Pride

Returning Pride

Lasting Pride

Serving Pride

Red Hot Christmas

My Sweet Valentine

Return To Me

Rescue Me

The Secret Series

Secret Seduction

Secret Pleasure

Secret Guardian

Secret Passions

Secret Identity

Secret Sauce

The West Series

Loving Lauren

Taming Alex

Holding Haley

Missy's Moment

Breaking Travis

Roping Ryan

Wild Bride

Corey's Catch

Tessa's Turn

The Grayton Series

Last Resort

Someday Beach

Rip Current

In Too Deep

Swept Away

High Tide

Lucky Series

Unlucky In Love

Sweet Resolve

Best of Luck

A Little Luck

Silver Cove Series

Silver Lining

French Kiss

Happy Accident

Hidden Charm

A Silver Cove Christmas

Entangled Series – Paranormal Romance

The Awakening

The Beckoning

The Ascension

Haven, Montana Series

Closer to You

Never Let Go

Holding On

Pride Oregon Series

A Dash of Love

My Kind of Love

Season of Love

Tis the Season

Dare to Love

Where I Belong

Wildflowers Series

Summer Nights

Summer Heat

Stand Alone Books

Twisted Rock

For a complete list of books:

http://JillSanders.com

ABOUT THE AUTHOR

Jill Sanders is a New York Times, USA Today, and international bestselling author of Sweet Contemporary Romance, Romantic Suspense, Western Romance, and Paranormal Romance novels. With over 55 books in eleven series, translations into several different languages, and audiobooks there's plenty to choose from. Look for Jill's bestselling stories wherever romance books are sold or visit her at jillsanders.com

Jill comes from a large family with six siblings, including an identical twin. She was raised in the Pacific Northwest and later relocated to Colorado for college and a successful IT career before discovering her talent for writing sweet and sexy page-turners. After Colorado, she decided to move south, living in Texas and now making her home along the Emerald Coast of Florida. You will find that the settings of several of her series are inspired by her time spent living in these areas. She has two sons and offset the testosterone in her house by adopting three furry little ladies that provide her company while she's locked in her writing cave. She enjoys heading to the beach, hiking, swimming, wine-tasting, and pickleball with her husband, and of course writing. If you have read any of her books, you may also notice that there is a love of food, especially sweets! She has been blamed for a few added pounds by her assistant, editor, and fans… donuts or pie anyone?

facebook.com/JillSandersBooks

twitter.com/JillMSanders

bookbub.com/authors/jill-sanders